MW00452495

WILD ROSE

Number 18
Clayton Wheat Williams Texas Life Series

WILD ROSE

§

The Life and Times of Victor Marion Rose,
Poet and Early Historian of Texas

Louise S. O'Connor

With Forewords by Gary Dunnam
and Margaret Stoner McLean

TEXAS A&M UNIVERSITY PRESS
COLLEGE STATION

This paper meets the requirements of ANSI/NISO Z39.48–1992
(Permanence of Paper).
Binding materials have been chosen for durability.
Manufactured in the United States of America

Library of Congress Cataloging-in-Publication Data

Names: O'Connor, Louise S., author.
Title: Wild Rose: the life and times of Victor Marion Rose, poet and early
    historian of Texas / Louise S. O'Connor; with forewords by Gary Dunnam
    and Margaret Stoner McLean.
Description: First edition. | College Station: Texas A&M University Press,
    [2018] | Series: Number 18: Clayton Wheat Williams Texas life series |
    Identifiers: LCCN 2018006361 (print) | LCCN 2018012420 (ebook) |
    ISBN 9781623496760 (ebook) | ISBN 9781623496753 | ISBN 9781623496753
    (cloth: alk. paper)
Subjects: LCSH: Rose, Victor M., 1842–1893. | Historians—Texas—Biography. |
    Newspaper editors—Texas—Biography. | Poets, American—Texas—Biography.
    | Texas—Biography.
Classification: LCC E175.5.R79 (ebook) | LCC E175.5.R79 O25 2018 (print) |
    DDC 976.4/06092 [B] —dc23

LC record available at https://lccn.loc.gov/2018006361

To
Margaret Stoner McLean and Kathryn Stoner O'Connor,
who spent their lives preserving the history of
the Rose and Stoner families

"[U]nfortunately much of the diversified minutiae from which a local work of this nature would be expected to derive a great deal of its interest, has been suffered to pass away like Autumn leaves; and that which should have been preserved with jealous care, until perpetuated upon the record, is irretrievably lost,—thus exemplifying the force of the trite, old maxim: What is the business of all is performed by none!"

—Victor Marion Rose, Preface to *History of Victoria County*

CONTENTS

FOREWORD

IN 1981 a friend gave me his late mother's copy of Victor Marion Rose's *History of Victoria County*. Having begun my college years as a history major, I found the 1961 reprint interesting, informative, and very wordy. The biographical sketches came to mean more to me as my interest in local history and family genealogy and connections expanded. I had no idea. . . .

It might help if I digress and give a little genealogy. Victor Rose's sister, Zilpa Rose, married George Overton Stoner. One of their daughters was Kathryn Carlisle Stoner. Kathryn married Tom O'Connor [III] (locals speak of him as Tom Sr.). From this union came Dennis, Mary, and Tom Jr. [IV]. It was Tom Jr. and his wife, Dorothy June "Junie" Broussard, who would give us Louise Stoner O'Connor.

In the late 1980s I introduced myself to Louise at Victoria's Nave Museum where an exhibit of her photography was on display. I was deeply moved by the images and expressed my thanks to her.

When our paths crossed again several years later and our friendship developed, Victor Rose's name came up more and more in our conversations across the dinner table. An attentive listener, she knew so much about him. It was fascinating to listen to those family stories. I had no idea. . . .

A few years ago Louise O'Connor proposed a reprint of all of her great-great-uncle's published writings. I offered to help in any way I could, mentioning my interest, specifically, in working on an annotated version of Rose's *History of Victoria County*. She welcomed me aboard, and I blithely walked the plank into the storm.

The last two years have been, for me, a voyage of discovery as I came to understand just how involved Victor Rose had been in the making of the history of Texas. A major part of this project has resulted in a biography of the man himself. Ms. O'Connor has produced a major work, not only of local interest, but one that touches so many aspects of nineteenth-century Texas history.

So, let's go back to Victoria and give Victor Rose's birth some context. The Great Comanche Raid—August 6, 1840—was still a lively topic of conversation in Victoria when Victor was born in 1842. Stumping for governor in 1857, Sam Houston delivered a three-hour speech under a blistering August sun on Diamond Hill, later attending a party at the home of Major A. H. Phillips across town. I would like to think that Victor and his father traveled from the Rose plantation five miles above Victoria to attend both events.

It was first on his father's knee that Victor learned the complex beauty of the English language. His works evidence an astounding vocabulary that enabled him to say *exactly* what he meant. It might be well to have your *Webster's Third Unabridged* at hand when you read his works. He did not misuse words!

Victor's military service in the Civil War left him a changed man. The studious, somewhat awkward young man came back to Victoria County wound as tightly as a coiled spring. He took his pen in hand and brought the bulk of his keen intelligence and curiosity, his remarkable knowledge of history, and his barbed wit into focus as author, poet, editor, publisher, and literary warrior. His writings are at their best when they force us to think about events and personalities in a new light. Rest assured, he regularly caught hell for it.

O'Connor's biography documents Victor Rose's life and career in detail. In addition to his combat experience, we follow him across Texas and back, from job to job. Running a newspaper was a much more exhausting task in Rose's day, at least in rural communities. There was no fleet of reporters scanning the countryside for bits of information and gossip. Rose was doing it all. As we read his newspaper editorials and essays, we come to realize how much more interesting newspapers were then versus now.

Indeed, the research and reading, the inclusion and exclusion was a long, drawn-out affair. But look what we have! Students of Texas history will find in these pages a compelling portrait of a notable but little-known Texas writer, as well as much new material about a complex era in the state's development.

Gary Dunnam
Victoria, Texas
January 2017

An Introduction to "Uncle Vic"

EARLY ON, I was absorbing miscellaneous historical facts about my family (and maybe some fiction) about those I never knew. On rare occasions when my mother, Mame Stoner Stoner, would be visiting her Victoria relatives, I would sometimes hear them talking about their uncle, Victor Rose. Victor Rose and Mayor John Henry Brown were contemporaries, friends, and they were both newspaper men. Victor was the editor of the *Victoria Advocate* from 1869 to 1873. He was also down in Laredo as editor of a newspaper there, The *Laredo Times*.[1]

The first time I heard his name, I was confused because I had an uncle named Victor Rose Stoner. He was not yet a priest, so I had to become an adult and know more family history before I could sort out the people with similar names. I can remember hearing "Other Mama," my grandmother, Zilpa Rose Stoner, telling my mother, Mame Stoner, about goings-on in Victoria and the family. We spent several weeks out at the ranch in the summers, and I would be sitting there just engrossed. I just wanted to listen. The cause of some of Uncle Vic's problems was spirits, which he apparently found too often. He was a legend in his time and especially in my family. I heard about him when I was growing up—a scandalous fellow, a romantic, and perhaps a ladies' man also.

From listening to these conversations, I got the impression that my great-uncle, at times, caused the family distress over some of his activities. I knew from talking to Mama (Mame Stoner Stoner)[2] and Aunt Kate (Kathryn Stoner O'Connor) that when they didn't want you to know anything, they just talked around it and you didn't hear it. At the same time, I knew that Aunt Kate thought he was a fine writer and historian who was not properly appreciated by those people of the present time who considered themselves writers and literary persons. And Uncle Victor was a Democrat to the hilt.

No one understood what he was saying most of the time. His language was flowery and from the era of the classics. No one had any faith in him. He was poetic and flighty. Everyone thought he was peculiar—he used certain phrases and big words. He had no idea how to work and was not an outdoor person.

He also wrote under the name "Wild Rose." Some of his writings were not signed, but his writing is so distinctive that you cannot mistake it for anyone but him. Uncle Vic wrote under a lot of noms de plume and wrote often about family weddings. And if they walked out the back door, he knew it and put it down in his columns and writings. In fact, he may have become a social pariah because of the Brooking marriage and the subsequent scandalous divorce.

The Roses were from the elite of England and then became part of the old gentry of the South. In the Old South, and almost forever after, they were elitists. A feeling prevailed that something was owed them—an attitude that came down from before the Civil War and grew worse after the war when so many strange people were among them.

Among the cognoscenti, they thought all Texans were ignoramuses. The Roses may not have attended Harvard or Yale, but they were educated. Uncle Vic learned from his father, and his education was based in the classics. He was one of the first literary figures in Texas, making him somewhat strange in a developing, frontier society. His phraseology and uncommon words are very recognizable in his writings.

Uncle Vic was a legend in his time and especially in my family. I heard about him often when I was growing up. The Roses were a volatile bunch, and Victor was considered strange by G. O. Stoner, his brother-in-law. He lived in another world, read all the time, stayed in the house, and wrote poetry. Victor was insular, stayed there and never left, so he was truly peculiar to those who were based in an agrarian culture.

Victor wrote about his times, giving us an eye into life in the South before and after the tragedy of the Civil War. One of his great talents was the ability to lead people into seeing the changing thinking of the times in his later works.

And Victor apparently ruptured the mores of his society often—indulging in inappropriate marriages, alcoholism, and chasing women. Family secrets were big at this time, so Victor was a source of scandal and gossip among the Victoria gentry. He often lived with his sister, Zilpa R. Stoner. His marriages and relationships with women never lasted long, and he stayed with family often.

Yet despite his scandals, Victor Rose influenced his family literarily down the line for several generations.[3] Descendent Anna Wellington Stoner also wrote in poetic language, using beautiful metaphors and word pictures.

He was not able to be discounted by the more proper, because he had written important historical works. He wrote of heroes and put his stamp on the history of that time by chronicling it and interpreting people's roles and their actions.[4]

Margaret Stoner McLean

PREFACE

VICTOR Marion Rose has always been something of a shadowy but prominent figure in my paternal side of the O'Connor family. He had a great influence on both the Stoner and O'Connor families. He was often referred to in my family as "Uncle Vic," and always in a slightly hushed tone—no one ever telling the full story—at least the more intimate aspects of it. References were made to a darker side, but very carefully. His story in my family was almost a "once upon a time there was a bad boy in our family" type reference that was introduced often into our discussions. He appears to be one of the earliest literary figures in Texas, something of a misfit in a family steeped in the Southern tradition, plantation life, slavery, the Civil War, and the "Lost Cause." They took their stance as Southerners quite seriously.

Uncle Vic has always fascinated me, even at a very young age, and only later in life did I realize his strong influence on the literary tendencies of my family. Through the generations, the O'Connor and Stoner families would use language much as Victor used. He was always around in the language and literary references constantly used in my family. In spite of being something of a rascal, he had left an imprint on future generations.

At times, he traveled and worked outside his home base, probably giving him a broader view of the world than was extant in the Victoria area in the 1800s. Although he stayed in the South, he achieved an objectivity that makes him important to study. He engaged in polemics in many areas, especially when he believed that history was being reported incorrectly, or that people were making untrue statements concerning the issues of the times. He was at once a journalist, literary writer, historian, classical writer, and poet, as well as a scholar. His works comprise manuscripts as well as critiques. He was a man of his time, and then a man of the changing times. He deviated often in later years from the normal views of history. Obsessed with preserving history and alternate views of history, he stayed in Texas and became objective in a time of great subjectivity.

Researching the life of Victor Marion Rose has been difficult, as some of his writings and commentary have been lost and much of the information is in widely scattered repositories (as listed in the bibliography). However, he is of enough value to Texas history and literature that I felt his story should be preserved and analyzed in a single volume. This work on Victor Marion Rose attempts to capture the essence of the man and his accomplishments, as well as the historical events that influenced him.

Special credit goes to my late cousin, Margaret Stoner McLean, who devoted much of her life to collecting and preserving the works of her great-uncle. Because of her skills as a researcher, as well as her place inside the Rose-Stoner family, she contributed invaluable input to this manuscript in its early stages. Although her health did not permit her later involvement in the project, her familiarity with Uncle Vic's writings and her knowledge of family lore made this book possible.

Thank you, Margaret.

WILD ROSE

Victor Marion Rose and His Times

VICTOR Marion Rose was many things: a prodigy, a bad boy, and a heroic survivor of the Civil War who suffered the loss of his entire culture and way of life. His father granted him an education that was both classical and useful; Rose was able to write complicated and interesting poetry, valuable historical accounts, and articles that appeared in newspapers all over Texas and the United States. This study of Victor Marion Rose reveals a previously little-known depth of thought, learning, and aesthetic sensibility. He was a historian and a poet, and he left behind an amazing assessment of the Old South and its way of life.

A Brief Review of Southern Culture

To truly appreciate Victor Marion Rose, it is first important to have a sense of the culture in which he was raised. A study of the Old South provides many of the clues needed to fit him into the overall pattern of Southern literature of the Civil War era in Texas and beyond.

Southerners were effective as orators and statesmen, but less so as deep thinkers who reached to examine the truth and critique the thoughts of others. Nevertheless, writing was a Southern avocation well before the Civil War, and during this period, when Rose had no need to make a living, he spent much of his time on writing and classical studies. The South had developed a romantic view of plantation life that discouraged much of the philosophical and theological speculation evident in New England transcendentalism, for example. Rather, most of those in positions of privilege in the Old South devoted themselves actively to the defense of a patriarchal system that they considered proper and noble.[1]

The chief defect of antebellum Southern poetry was artificiality. The prose was too natural and was not subtle or refined, though it presumably gave delight to people of its day. Much of it is almost unreadable today, but it did represent the life of the people it portrayed, even to the point of caricature. The stated political hallmark of the South was states' rights, championed by a class that has been described as belonging to the Episcopal Church, voting the Whig ticket, and reading Sir Walter Scott.[2]

W. J. Cash makes some comments that are useful in understanding the Old South,[3] describing it, as do most historians, as "a plantation culture, bound by a number of social, economic, and political factors— slavery, cotton, plantations, a decentralized and agrarian existence. They also tirelessly defended southern society and slavery."[4] The agricultural nature of the South is also fundamental to understanding its character, practices, lifestyle, and attitudes. This setting was central to Rose's life as a child and young man.

The South clung to slave labor, believing it necessary to remain competitive with the North. Later, this insistence on a slave culture would bring the South down when the institution was abolished. Hypocrisy and artifice were rampant in the land before and after the Civil War. Yet there was rural security and a type of beauty in affluent Southern lives. James Kirke Paulding notes: "The Southern culture was pervaded by a love of country life over urban ways. They felt the speculation and capitalistic ways of the north were corrupting."[5] Rose, of course, would live through the profound destruction of this culture.

By 1850 the South was viewed by the North as aristocratic and violent, given to social pretensions and economic backwardness. It was, in fact, steeped in a deeply conservative ethos. Free thinking and unconventional behavior were frowned upon in the South, especially among the gentry and the planter classes. These circumstances caused problems for Rose from an early age.

The white Southern worldview was intertwined with slavery. White Southerners believed that slaves deserved their status because of their race. The masters defended this view with quotations from the Old and New Testaments: "Slaves, obey your earthly masters in everything; and do it, not only when their eye is on you and to curry their favor, but with sincerity of heart and reverence for the Lord" (Colossians 3:22).

While the North evolved away from the ideals of primal, clan-based honor and toward more private, personal manifestations of "integrity," the South held onto the tenets of traditional honor for a much longer period of time. The Southern code of honor borrowed from notions of the medieval honor code of Europe—combining the reflexive, violent honor code of primitive man with the public virtue and chivalry of knights. This required the Southern man to have a reputation of honesty and integrity, self-sufficiency, and mastery of his household. He needed a willingness to use violence to defend any perceived slight to his reputation, as a man of integrity, strength, and courage. He was also required to defend any threats to his independence and kin. Even if a man were guilty of something, the ability to dominate or kill someone who impugned his honor meant his reputation might remain intact.

Such conceptions of classical honor survived in the South, even as they became less dominant in the North because of cultural differences in the early settlers and the divergent cultures of the two regions. The earliest European settlers in the North were primarily farmers from more established European countries such as the Netherlands, Germany, and urban England. The South was settled primarily by farmers and herdsmen from the more rural and undomesticated parts of the British Isles. This in turn created different cultures with starkly different notions of honor. Among the herdsman-dominated culture, it was essential to have the strength and willingness to use violence to protect one's herds and to deter attackers. The Irish, who also settled much of the South, exemplify the warrior-herder societies. Constituting half of the South's population by 1860, the Irish not only brought with them their penchant for herding, but also brought their love of whiskey, music, leisure, gambling, and hunting. Although Texas had its own culture based on frontier and ranch life, it was heavily imbued with many attributes of the Old South and the cultures noted. The Rose Plantation fit perfectly into this picture.[6]

After their defeat in the Civil War, many of the former plantation owners and others who had been among the Southern elite likely considered their lives to be wretched and miserable, but they refused, in many cases, to change in order to make a new life in this strange world.

History asserts that Lincoln tried several times to work with the South to make the transition easier and less devastating for all, but his suggestions and plans were rejected.[7] Another grave mistake was thus made, and Victor Marion Rose did not miss the point of this. Further, Rose's criticism of Jefferson Davis is easily backed up by history's take on him and his leaders. Because Rose did change some of his ways of thinking, openly criticized Southern policies that he perceived as detrimental, and forged a path through the altered landscape of the Reconstruction South, he was considered rather unusual, both in postwar Texas society in general and within his family in particular.

The Old South loved a good scandal, and almost every deviation from what was considered the norm would feed gossip and create a new topic of interest, each breathlessly awaited, just as many hang onto celebrity culture today. With his unconventional views and eloquent writing, Rose quickly assumed the role as topic of conversation—a "celebrity" of his day.

The Old South and Victor Marion Rose

One of Rose's greatest attributes was embracing objectivity in a time of great subjectivity during the era of the Civil War and after. He became a man of his time, but in a much different way from many who refused to give up the Old South and the Confederacy. He realistically analyzed the era and did not back down from facing the mistakes made by the South. Bankruptcy after the war required Rose to make his own living. In spite of the fact that men of letters and scholarly pursuits were considered almost useless after the war, he pulled himself up and engaged in a career of newspaper work and earned a living. He founded several newspapers and was an editor for the *Laredo Times*. On occasion he would engage in introspection in his poetry, his newspaper columns, and biographies, but true to the times that often lacked this practice, he also often left introspection to others.

His choices of subject matter and viewpoints are interesting. He was working from an isolated culture, but his classical education gave him a much broader scope than was normal for Southern writers at the time. Industrialism was changing the literature of the North, but the South did not have as much access to this input, creating literary limitations. In many cases, literary pursuits took a back seat to oratory.[8] Blustery and belligerent, many Southerners seemed to be always on guard for some infraction against their code of honor, any imagined insult, or threat to their way of life.

Readers should note that Rose himself bought into the predominant beliefs of his class and culture, at least for a time. He often bemoaned the "Lost Cause," and yet at the same time evidenced a realistic view of the foolhardy actions of the South as he went to work after the war. Reading his work, one is prompted to ask: Did he at some time truly believe in the South and then see the foolish and destructive beliefs and actions that brought it down, or did he simply change his writing for public consumption in accordance with the newfound enlightenment of the postwar situation? There is, regrettably, no way to know this for sure.

His biographies, though containing some elements of hero worship, offer an amazing source of historical perspective. He knew the people, participated in the events of history, and lived in an era of spectacular feuds and notable happenings. Living the life of a Southern gentleman, supposedly one of kindness, conscientiousness, chivalry,[9] and noblesse oblige toward inferiors, he nevertheless participated in one of the worst wars in history. He lived through the terrible times after that war that forced him into a position of needing to write, not as an observer, but as a participant in history as it was being made.

If one reads only Rose's early works, one might assume that he followed the hopeless, emotional mess of the Southern cause. Only upon reading his histories and biographies does the reader realize that he may quite possibly have been against secession, as is commonly believed today. He fully understood the situation, relating often and well to the reason that it was a "Lost Cause." His honesty in analyzing slavery, the reasons for eventual secession, and the incompetence of the Confederate government in spite of strong and brilliant military leaders is quite stunning. He absolutely "got it," while at the same time having sympathy and empathy for the situation of the South.

Rose helped keep the South alive for a time after the war by organizing and engaging in tournaments after the Civil War that were designed to keep some of the traditions of the Old South, such as chivalry, alive and well. They were attempts to heal the wounds of loss and assuage the crushing grief felt by many Southerners.[10] They were romantic and entertaining and served as distractions for a radically altered society. However, they appeared to be of great importance to those steeped in the causes of the South. Rose was one of the main organizers of these gatherings and also wrote most of the poems and speeches connected with them.[11]

Thus far, Rose's invaluable insights into the eras before, during, and after the Civil War have been largely ignored in analysis and assessments of his works. What is known, however, is that few in the South shared the opinions Rose expressed publicly after the war. Many of his positions went against popular opinion or were embarrassing to his family, considered simply not appropriate for public discussion. Yet one might be reasonably persuaded that he truly believed what he wrote, especially since it caused him much trouble later in his life.

A Person of Many Faults

In Victor Marion Rose's time, women were mystical Southern belles: worshiped, but held firmly in their place. Southern pride was based in masculinity, an attribute Victor seemed to lack, according to some of his contemporaries. Along this line, Rose's writings displayed contradictions with his actual behavior at times, which was less than gentlemanly. There was a collective temperament in the South affirming that a woman's job was to soften society. Rose wrote often of this softer side, but would also write about powerful women. However, he often treated women as objects, and this behavior alienated a number of "decent" women from his attentions in his personal life.

At times, Rose was not above using and abusing the less virtuous women he encountered. He wrote romantically about women, but did not always behave in a way that was commensurate with his writings, engaging in bizarre and often obsessive relationships, often with more than one woman.[12] When drinking, Rose's treatment of his former wife, Ada Brooking, exhibited a much different stance than his flowery, chivalric poetry might lead us to assume. Due in part, no doubt, to this contradiction, true happiness seems to have eluded him all his life.

Notwithstanding all this, a careful observer or biographer may often observe that personal flaws do not prevent a person from producing beautiful and valuable work. Many a "bad boy" before and after Victor Marion Rose have produced great literature. He offers invaluable insight in his reports of the cataclysmic events through which he lived.

Ostracizing Victor Marion Rose

Even after the war, the white pastoral culture of honor remained in the South, with its emphasis on courage, strength, and violence (when necessary), often augmented by wariness toward outsiders. Thus white Southern culture understood, ascribed to, and enforced its honor code, making Rose subject to shunning by society when his choices violated the tenets of the code. Being an outcast was one of the worst fates that could befall a proper, white Southerner. For this reason, Rose's postwar stances on the culture and history of the South, including his growing disavowal of slavery, cost him dearly at times. Many of Rose's published views shocked his family.[13] He was questioned for living a life of the mind, as Philip Pendleton Cooke in "Florence Vane" stated: "Why do you waste your time on a damned thing like poetry? A man of your position could be a useful man."[14]

Many other Southerners of divided loyalties made the same choice as Robert E. Lee.[15] United in opposition to the encroachment of outsiders, the perceived threat to their autonomy, and the necessity of demonstrating honor by adopting an aggressive stance and fighting when insulted, the vast majority of white Southerners, whether slave owners or not, took up arms for the Confederacy. Because of their shared honor code, there was, at least at first, a great deal of unity in the "Old South." There were fewer socioeconomic clashes of the type that arose between the "gentlemen" and the "roughs" in the Union Army.[16] When, in his postwar writing, Rose diverged from this solidarity, he did so at great cost to his personal reputation among his peers and family.

Rose went Populist, moving away from his family's elitism. He began writing about the problems of farmers and berating the elite who held power.[17] The previous isolation had not served the South or the Rose family well in the end, and Rose did not hesitate to take note of it.[18] His belief that the assassination of Lincoln was the gravest mistake the South could have made was another unusual attitude for the time. Lincoln was detested by Southerners and considered by many to be the cause of all their problems.

Rose stated his unpopular views unabashedly and without restraint. He often wrote with great sympathy and empathy about the many aspects of the situation of the South before, during, and after the war from a genuine and critical standpoint. His postwar writings soon began to show his objectivity and criticism of the cause of the South and its leaders.

It is likely that his views on the Civil War, freed African Americans, and other social issues of the day may have done as much to make him an object of scandal as his abusive, alcoholic behavior. In the South Texas culture of Rose's youth and in the family that raised him, eschewing the Confederacy was heresy and treason, in spite of the fact that there were Unionists in Texas, one being Thomas O'Connor [I], whose progeny was to become a Rose descendent.[19] Opposition in any way to "The Cause" could bring not only social ostracism but even violence to the offender. Thus running counter to these stances was a brave move on his part.

Aside from Rose's political views, his personal life—particularly his love life—also led him to be ostracized from his family and proper society. It is hard to tell why he chose to consort with a strange assortment of women. However, many of the more decent ones seem to have fled from him, while others were of the lower echelons of society and reputation from the start. Yet he wrote of women in the most endearing way: "It is not the smile of a pretty face, the delicate tint of complexion, the luring glance of the eye, the beauty, symmetry of person, nor costly dress or decorations that compose a woman's beauty. It is her pleasing deportment, her chaste conversation, the sensibility and purity of her thoughts, her affable and open disposition, her sympathy for those in adversity, her comfort and relief to the distressed, and about all, her humility, that constitutes true loveliness."[20] This aside, Victor was seemingly attracted to women apparently not imbued with the ethics espoused in his writings and certainly did not abide by these musings in his treatment of his second wife, which led him to be ostracized even further from gentlemanly Southern society.

Consequences of Nonconformity

The Roses were from the ruling class in England and, it is said, married into the gentlefolk of America, such as the Washington family.[21] The rules and mores of the South were those of the Rose family. They never gave up, they never adjusted, and they never "got over it." In the traditional code of honor, loyalty to one's group or clan takes precedence over all other demands—even those of one's own conscience. Much to his credit, Victor Marion Rose departed from these family norms. While his earlier writings convey a desire to return to an aristocratic, agricultural past, his views and his writing changed over time.

Victor was apparently somewhat complacent and detached before the Civil War. Then the reality of the whole thing came down on him hard. However, he was able to rise above the despair and work to make a living. It should be noted that there was a time after the war when he was still pining and grieving, unable to get his feet on the ground. His was not an immediate recovery from the fantasy. He also was not engaged in the reality of life on a plantation as far as the work, the animals, and the crops were concerned. His previous life of ease stymied his attempts at working the plantation after the war.

He was a man who, under other circumstances, could have inherited, but his inheritance[22] was destroyed by the losses created by the Civil War. He chose instead to make a living with his talent for writing, though it was unusual for educated gentry to go to work after the war. His writings give us an amazing look into how the gentry, however few, survived. Some Confederates—at least the men—were crippled for generations afterward. If they learned to work with their hands, they were forever resentful or shamed by their less than gentlemanly situation.[23] This statement would apply strongly to members of the Rose family—with the exception of Victor Marion Rose—for several generations to follow.[24]

Some have asserted that during Reconstruction the North set out to destroy any remnant of the Southern mind.[25] Victor appeared steeped in a lack of reality about the Southern cause in his early life and writings. Yet he was able to break away from these attitudes as the reality of loss and necessity of making a living came down heavily on the South and his family. We may notice Rose beginning to remove himself from certain delusions about the Old South and making a monumental change in order to survive. He threw off the mantle of martyrdom, rejecting the role of propagandist for the Old South, even as his family continued its allegiance to the "Lost Cause."

Mining Rose's work reveals unusual attitudes for the times regarding African Americans, Lincoln, the Civil War, and Confederate leaders. He was opposed to secession, yet he joined the Confederacy. Early on, he displays paternalistic attitudes toward the slaves, considering them fit only for slavery. Later, we see him begin to respect them as they advance themselves after Emancipation. He progressed through time in his thoughts and beliefs about the freed slaves. "The only thing necessary to make a good citizen of 'Our Brother in Black' is just treatment, and where this has been accorded them, possibly, the percentage of lawlessness has been less among them than with other classes. In every instance in which they have given trouble elsewhere, investigation has revealed designing white men as the instigators."[26] In January 1888, he makes note of a number of lynchings and killings of blacks in the North. It cannot be known if he was just reporting the news or if he was trying to make a point about the North and its true treatment of blacks, while spewing piety about the whole situation.

Throughout his writings, he would drift into details about the South that were extremely accurate. His ability to drop these pearls of wisdom into the mix showed remarkable intellect and objectivity that was rare for the times. He wrote of the military leaders as heroes while criticizing the government leaders as wanting in their jobs. He even announces that the Civil War was a huge mistake and totally unnecessary. "There was never a more causeless war—and a fearful responsibility for its consequences rests on the Yankee abolitionists."[27]

It would be interesting to see if he could have been as productive if he hadn't had to struggle to make a living after the war. Actually, the fact that he was forced to go to work, and had the good sense and courage to do that rather than sit around after the Civil War, "howling like a hound dog sitting on grass burrs,"[28] as did much of his family, must surely have made him a more productive writer. Either way, Rose should be reconsidered as a viable, valuable chronicler of his times.

An Insight into Victor Marion Rose's Writing

While examining Rose's writings, we must consider the fact that he was well known beyond the boundaries of Texas, as some of his writings appeared across the United States. His newspaper columns often appeared outside of Texas. His work as a historian and general literary figure at a time when literary pursuits were not held in high esteem demonstrate his perseverance. He attempted to preserve history and culture in all of his works, and possibly contributed somewhat to opening minds in a tightly closed culture that was stubbornly resistant to or incapable of deep reflection and analysis.

Rose, in his writings, showed that he had great range, writing in genres from ephemeral poetry to history and biography. He covered an amazing number of subjects. His passion was to create an overall history of his times as well as to give his readers a glimpse into classical literature and history. He was dedicated to bringing down assumed heroes who were not actually heroes. He was a myth buster, making him vulnerable to social ostracism for undermining the South's view of itself that pervaded the South in the Civil War era. His excoriation of the leaders of the Confederacy was remarkable for his time. His biographies are thorough and delve deeply into the lives of individuals and subject matter. His relating of historical events as witnessed by participants, himself included, is invaluable.

In his correspondence and his newspaper work, he became a great promoter of Texas and engaged in pushing for the state's development and settlement. He wrote of heroes such as Ben McCulloch and L. S. "Sul" Ross, great war generals. Both were examples of those who returned from war and lived quiet and peaceful lives, just as Rose did.[29]

He greatly admired McCulloch, who was much loved by his men because of his "humanity" and "noble nature."[30] Victor often wrote of how others got on after the war, noting that many who returned never got back on their feet, while others pulled themselves together and went on with life, such as the Honorable O. N. Hollingsworth.[31] He notes that many summoned up "indomitable will, energy, and pluck" and "entered the race of life again."[32] Admittedly, Rose did romanticize the world that was lost by defeat in the Civil War. He wrote of and from his true time and place in the world as well as his circumstances. But ultimately, the sudden poverty of the South caused him to go to a more realistic place in his writing.[33]

In Rose's *History of Victoria County*, almost every page reveals some statement or thought bearing witness to unpopular truths. For example, while his take on slaves was definitely paternalistic and he viewed them as inferiors, he also thoughtfully notes that the lack of education for slaves could have made them appear as inferior beings to others. Following emancipation, Rose specifically enunciates the problem of lack of education for former slaves. A decade or two after the end of the war, Rose begins writing about freedmen who were making accomplishments in society.[34] His pen identifies many freedmen quickly rising and achieving as soon as they had some means of educating themselves. In one particular article in *The Old Capitol*, he praises an accomplished black man.[35]

Rose also wrote of the people he considered worthy of remembering, and in his poetry he recorded his feelings and memories about a time and a place. Despite his progression in thought, he remained ever Southern in sensibility, and in some of his descriptions of what the South went through during Reconstruction, his rancor and rage were certainly understandable. This makes his ability to take a more open-minded look at the South even more remarkable, as life in the South after Reconstruction was uncertain at best.[36] His purpose in producing these works seems to have come from a deep need to write. In his 1882 preface to *Demara*, a volume of poetry, he says that he has "been possessed of a chronic case of *cacoethes scribendi*[37] since I can well remember."[38] The subject matter he chose became a lucid and interesting record of his classical education, the times, and his very serious interest in recording the history of a savage war.

Rose had a great influence on literary knowledge and understanding in his family for several generations to follow. Throughout the O'Connor and Stoner family collections, papers can be found reflecting a tradition of writing that begins in childhood and extends into later life. Family members often wrote poetry to each other, sent funny messages back and forth down the hallway during siblings' convalescences, and mailed funny drawings and letters from school, pleading to come home. All showed a proficiency in writing and communicating on paper, and it is not difficult to see how Rose's heritage and talent for writing was passed down through the generations. Indeed, lines from his poetry and prose were often used as a means of communication within both families for several generations.

Rose's works remain relevant. Many of the issues he wrote about are being restudied by modern scholars, and some of his views sound surprisingly current. Others may criticize his more inflammatory musings, and yet his work is once again being used as a primary resource. Thomas Cutrer wrote on Ben McCulloch, following Rose's study of a century earlier. Gregg Cantrell[39] also uses Rose as a source, albeit taking something of a negative view of his assault on Stephen F. Austin in his work *In the Balances*. Cantrell referred to this work as "splenic." Nevertheless, these mentions of Rose by today's scholars serve to bring him into the world of relevant writers of history.[40]

Rose's continued relevance is a strong indication that his words were of value in his time and certainly are valuable to us now. His range was amazing, and he was obsessed with making sure history was recorded and reported accurately. He would also engage in polemics with other writers he felt were not being accurate. He admired his heroes and was relentless in attacking his real and perceived enemies, all the while writing beautiful words and thoughts in his poetry. Plagued by numerous demons, he seems to have used them, as writers often do, to create his poetry. Coming from a long line of contentious, wild men in the Rose family, it is no wonder that these genes were also residing in Victor Marion Rose.

He reveals his private view of life and shows how the educated gentry got on with life after the war. He gives us a great view of the Old South before and after the war. He was a literary figure who covered so many areas, also having the courage to engage in polemics in politics and other daily happenings. He was journalistic, he was artistic, he was a war hero and a bit of an iconoclast, and was one of the few people that could write about the times from an insider's perspective.

CHAPTER ONE

The Formative Years

1842–1860

VICTOR ROSE was born during the era of the Republic of Texas, giving him a chance to see Texas change from a wild frontier to a more settled society. As Texas made progress and became more civilized, settlers adopted the agrarian ways of the South. This agrarian plantation life supported by slavery was part and parcel of Victor's youth.

He was born in Victoria at the family home on "Diamond Hill" on October 1, 1842.[1] When the Roses first arrived in Victoria, they lived in the southeast quadrant of the original town plat. The hill overlooked the flats of the Guadalupe River, and later in the century became an exclusive part of town that was home to doctors, lawyers, and prosperous merchants. At this time, however, Victoria, then known as Guadalupe Victoria, was "a miserable little hamlet of jacals."[2] With a population numbering only several hundred people, the town had recently defended itself against one of the largest Comanche raids in Texas.

Victor was the third of thirteen children of John Washington Rose and Margaret Scott Rose, and the eldest son to reach maturity. He had numerous characters pass through his life, either in his family or in some way involved with his family. Numerous family members were noted in history, or more accurately were infamous.

Victor's great-grandfather was John Fredrick Rose, a veteran of the American Revolution. His great-grandmother, Mary Washington Rose, was a niece of our nation's first president, George Washington. Victor's grandfather was William Pinckney Rose, known as Captain Rose and "Hell Roarin'" Rose,[3] who fought in the Battle of New Orleans under Gen. Andrew Jackson. He was also a member of Mississippi's constitutional convention, later served in the Mississippi legislature, and became a prosperous planter.

The Rose family had come from Surrey, England, in the 1600s.[4] No specific details are known about their history in England other than they were reported by family legend to be of the gentry.[5]

In May 1839, William Pinckney Rose moved to the area now known as Harrison County, Texas, bringing with him a large group, including his wife, their children, married children with their spouses and children and many in-laws. They arrived, unfortunately, just at the time that the Regulator-Moderator War was about to reach the shooting stage, and it was inevitable that Rose and his group would become involved. Rose soon became the acknowledged leader of the Regulators, a role that not only cost him his quite considerable fortune, but also caused the death of a son-in-law, George W. Rembert. Also lost was Isaac Hughes, the brother of another son-in-law, both killed by Moderators, whose leader was Robert Potter.[6]

Thus began the famous feud known as the Rose-Potter feud.[7] It was an interesting enough event and of sufficient historical importance to be chronicled in a novel, *Love Is a Wild Assault*, by Elithe Hamilton Kirkland.[8]

Potter was endowed with a brilliant mind and energetic, fearless spirit, but he also had an explosive temperament and was feared and hated by his enemies. He signed the Declaration of Independence, was a framer of the Constitution, and first secretary of the Republic's navy. He became a legend. Born of a good family in modest circumstances in North Carolina in 1800, he was supportive of blacks and the lower classes, which scared the aristocracy.

Both Potter and Rose were involved in the Regulator–Moderator War. In the winter of 1839, William Pinckney Rose and his family moved to Louisiana Texas as the vigilante group, the Regulators, were attempting to preserve law and order in the no-man's-land around the Sabine River to the Gulf. In the meantime, the excesses of the Regulators became so bad that the Moderators were formed to control the Regulators.

Rose was the leader of the Regulators, a man of many adventures and exploits and a legendary figure in his community, an image he encouraged or created for himself. He claimed he had served under Andrew Jackson in the Battle of New Orleans in 1812 and said he was at a meeting with Jackson and the pirate Jean Lafitte. Jackson's memoirs do not indicate this. Rose called himself a captain and was only in the military for about two months.

Potter was apparently the leader in the Moderator's camp and was opposed to Rose's wild ways and methods. Rose was a bully and loved to be called "The Lion of the Lake." To further add to the friction, Rose had supported an opponent of Potter's, Daniel Turner, in an election for the Senate.

In addition, Rose and Potter, once friends, had fallen out over some land on the north shore of the lake in Panola County. When Potter rode home, he had apparently made up his mind to deal with Rose, who was under indictment by a Harrison County grand jury. After this land dispute at Rose's home, Potter was followed to his house and killed by Rose's men, who were led by Rose himself.

The death of Potter put an end to the bloody strife of the Rose-Potter feud. However, Potter continued to influence Texas long after his death. Potter had argued in the US Congress about the question of tariffs on salt imports, creating a strong case for Texas then and into modern times. It allowed her boundaries to extend three leagues from shore. Even before the Texas Navy was created, Potter was authorized to range throughout the Gulf of Mexico looking for the Navy. This permission was later used by Texas concerning oil and gas deposits offshore in the Gulf. Texas was able to claim great stretches of Gulf waters and the mineral wealth as belonging to Texas, not the United States. The Republic's operations in the Gulf under Potter apparently carried great weight later, and Texas was awarded three leagues seaward. The Gulf became a "Texas Lake" thanks to Potter.[9]

Like other sons who came from a long line of well-connected individuals with distinguished records of military service and civic leadership, Victor's father, John Washington Rose, a Louisiana native, was sent off to school for a proper education. He graduated from Mississippi College, in Clinton, Mississippi, and in 1837 he received a law degree from the South's leading institution of higher learning, Transylvania College in Lexington, Kentucky.[10] Soon he was practicing law in Gallatin, Mississippi, the county seat of Copiah County at that time.[11]

On May 24, 1838, he married Margaret Malinda Scott of Copiah County. In 1839 their first child was born, and died before his second birthday. In the fall of 1841 they relocated to Victoria, which had grown from a colony founded in 1824 on the Guadalupe River by the Mexican empresario Martin De Leon. Rose served as chief justice of Victoria County from 1842 to 1846, an indication that he was not only an influential figure in town, but was also well regarded among the Republic's statesmen. Chief justices at this time were elected by both houses of the Republic of Texas Congress. Along with a promising career, he had a growing family, which included Victor.

When Victor Marion was born, he became the eldest son in the family and was named for Victor DuGaillon, a Frenchman who lived with the Rose family for many years.[12] Victor grew up surrounded by educated, sophisticated people who were prominent and productive citizens; their influence helped foster his innate intelligence and curiosity.[13]

After the annexation of Texas in 1846, John Rose was chosen to represent Victoria in the House of Representatives in the First Texas Legislature, a position he held from February 16, 1846, until December 13, 1847. During this time, he served as chair of the Land Office Committee and as a member of several select House committees, his party affiliation being listed as "Democrat."[14]

Whereas politics prior to annexation had centered on personalities, statehood brought with it the party structure that characterized national politics. Most Texans regarded themselves as Democrats because this was the party that had supported annexation.[15] It should be noted that annexation not only had been considered after the Revolution, but had been proven to be an end result all along, even before the Texas Revolution.[16]

Soon after arriving in Austin in 1846, John Rose, in writing to his wife,[17] was clearly homesick. In March he wrote to say that the session was expected to adjourn in mid-April, adding "I don't think I can hold out longer."[18] According to the Victoria County tax rolls for 1846 and 1847, John Rose owned three parcels of land on the Guadalupe River, totaling about two thousand acres that were probably badly in need of his attention.

By September 1847, John Rose, "in quest of health," had relocated with his family to the newly established port town of Saluria on Matagorda Island in Calhoun County.[19] He suffered from chronic respiratory ailments for most of his adult life. A niece later noted that he "was always moving looking for some climate that suited him."[20] Surely the climate of the Texas coast could not have been good for him. In the diary of Zilpa Rose Stoner, John's daughter and Victor's sister, there is an entry about how they traveled from Saluria to Victoria. Victor would have lived an insular life in this insular area as a young boy. He left no writings of any memory of this trip or his life on the coast as a toddler.

In Saluria, John was associated with Robert J. Clow, a merchant who sold dry goods, groceries, hardware, and "fancy articles," but the extent of John's involvement in the business is not known.[21] He may have also been engaged in legal work. In the 1850 census for Calhoun County he listed his occupation as "lawyer." According to his assets, he was certainly affluent if not wealthy during Victor's early childhood. They had lived with all that entailed, including a large coterie of servants. Yet John was apparently aloof and not a warm and nurturing figure, in spite of his considerable wealth and education.[22]

Victor's first teacher, according to an account that he wrote in 1888 after visiting Matagorda, was Elizabeth M. Rice Stapp. Describing the visit, he said: "We had the pleasure of meeting our much loved first teacher, Mrs. Hugh Stapp, née Miss Lizzie Rice, at whose knee we solved the intricate problem of 'A.B.C.' That was a long time ago, but 'Miss Lizzie' looked almost as young as when a pretty young school

marm, she wielded with dexterous aim the fatal slipper upon the cor-
porosity of refractory urchins. Deal gently with her, O, Time! is the
prayer of him who perhaps collided more frequently with the slipper
than any one else."[23]

This comment about the slipper is an interesting peep into Victor's
later reputation, as he apparently was in trouble in school from an early
age. We also see that Victor spent some of his early childhood along the
coast and not on the large plantation near Victoria. This full Southern
plantation lifestyle was to come a little later when his family moved to
"Forest Grove."[24]

As we have seen, he received much of his education from his father,
who imparted to his son most of the classical curriculum that he himself had absorbed at Mississippi College. That became the wellspring
for the classical allusions and erudite references in Victor's writings. As
historian, David Sansing explains, educators in the antebellum South
believed that"[a] thorough grounding in the classics was the best means
of managing, training, and disciplining the mind. . . . Consequently,
antebellum students took a prescribed course of study in Latin and
Greek, ancient history and literature, philosophy, logic rhetoric, and the
'evidences of Christianity.' The classical curriculum and its corollary, the
'genteel tradition,' were based on the assumption that a classical education produced Christian gentlemen and that Greek and Latin were
necessary for an understanding of that grand body of knowledge that
was 'the substance of western civilization.'"[25]

In addition to reading Greek and Latin translations of the Bible,[26]
John Rose, at this point a judge, immersed himself in news of current
affairs. Victor's brother, John Jr., would later recount that their father
had been a subscriber of the *Galveston Daily News* from its inception,
that their mother had also been a dedicated reader of the paper, and that
he himself had read it"since I could read anything." He remembered that
during the war, the family subscribed to the *Houston Telegraph* and the
San Antonio Herald, as well as the Galveston paper.[27] This habit of Judge
Rose must have exposed Victor to journalism early in life.

The Rose household was an environment that fostered respect for
the written word, and evidently Victor showed a literary bent early

on, trying his hand at writing stories and poems. A handwritten note in the family papers says, "Even as a small boy he was always making r[hy]mes, to the other children."[28] Regrettably, none of these appear to have survived.

The relationship between Victor and his father is not known on the personal level, but Judge Rose may have been a forbidding and demanding figure. According to sister Zilpa, "Papa always rode over the field every evening. He never left his room before noon. We children were not allowed in the house, as the childish noise disturbed him. So you can see that we knew very little about him, and when we were near him, we were afraid to speak."[29] It should be noted that in spite of the somewhat strange sense of humor in the family, there was also a taciturn, if not ill-tempered, aspect that came down through the generations.

Victor was the only one of the Rose children who was favored with an elite education—for the other children were sent to local and county schools. Perhaps he was given this opportunity because he presented as more intelligent or interested in learning than his siblings. An incorrigible bookworm, Victor had no aptitude or inclination for the work involved in rural life, and he was considered a "sissy" by the other children.

Some accounts suggest that Victor may also have attended private boarding schools in Victoria for brief periods, the private school of Mr. Kilgore[30] in 1848, and Mr. Norton's in 1851. He also attended Rutersville College in Fayette County for one term, presumably when he was in his early teens, perhaps in 1855 or 1856.[31] Organized by the widely known pioneer Methodist missionary Martin Ruter and other Methodists, the college was chartered in 1840 and located in the community of Rutersville near present-day La Grange. With such close ties to the Methodist church, the college was no doubt selected for Victor by his father, a staunch Methodist. Victor was raised in a faith-filled household, and references to a higher power frequently appear in his writing. His early religious training instilled a morality in him that is evident later in life in his poems, especially "Demara" and "Perdu," bemoaning his constant fall from grace in spite of trying to control himself.[32] Thus, the faith-based institute of Rutersville provided the perfect setting for Victor's journey into formal higher education.

Rutersville offered courses of study in the following departments: "moral science," belles lettres, mathematics, ancient languages, literature, and modern languages. There was also a Preparatory Department and a Female Department. Because of the stringent requirements for admission to the degree-level courses (including Davies's algebra, ancient and modern geography, Latin and Greek grammar, Caesar's *Commentaries,* Cicero's *Select Orations, The Georgics* and *Aeneid* of Virgil, and Jacob's Greek reader or St. John's gospel in Greek), most of the students entered the Preparatory Department. The academic year was divided into two terms of twenty-one weeks each, followed by a five-week vacation.[33] It is unknown which department Victor entered under, but regardless he had studied much of the curricula earlier at his father's knee, surely making him more acceptable to the faculty than many of his peers. He was now living in a world more suited to his personality and abilities.

Victor was a pupil of Reverend Homer S. Thrall,[34] a leading Methodist in the region who served as president of the college and went on to become an author of schoolbooks on Texas history. Later, Victor would attack Thrall's *History* as appallingly inaccurate.[35] It remains unknown why Victor stayed at Rutersville for only one term; perhaps he left of his own accord or was asked to leave because of unsatisfactory academic performance or "ungentlemanly" deportment.

Needless to say, this coeducational school setting would have afforded Victor an opportunity to fraternize with young ladies without the watchful eye of his father. Even though the young men and ladies of Rutersville were taught in a separate building, we know that his romantic entanglements began in his youth. In fact, when he was only fourteen, he fell in love with a flirtatious widow more than twice his age who had come to visit his mother. When the woman left, Victor followed her and had to be forcibly returned home by Judge Rose.[36] This wasn't an isolated incident; according to family lore and quite a proven historical record, Victor's susceptibility to women's charms often landed him in hot water. His passionate and perhaps outrageous actions at times passed beyond the normal rebellious behavior of a willful youth.[37] At an early age, it was clear: Victor was remarkably different and perhaps even troubled.

But whatever his demons were, they did not prevent him from turning out valuable history and poetry.

The Roses left Saluria in 1851 and returned to Victoria with two additional children in the family, Zilla and Zilpa, born in 1848 and 1850, respectively. After traveling up the Guadalupe River on a small steamboat named the *Lizzie Lane*, the family first settled about thirteen miles below Victoria.[38] Then, in September 1851, John Rose paid early settler Jesse O. Wheeler $5,000 for a league of land, slightly less than 4,500 acres, located on the left bank of the river about five miles above Victoria.[39] They had yet to establish a large plantation, but it was soon to be the family's home.

John Rose's younger brother, Preston Robinson Rose, also settled in the area, described as a "pretty rough character, a Texas Cowboy, pure and simple." He purchased 12,000 acres, known as "Buena Vista," about nine miles south of Victoria on the Guadalupe River. His wife, Mary Ann Scott Rose, was a sister of John Rose's wife, Margaret Scott Rose. Their six children had many occasions to play with their Forest Grove cousins, with the two Rose families living in proximity to each other.[40]

The Rose family continued to grow in the 1850s. John Washington was born on March 19, 1853; Margaret Malinda on April 13, 1855; Mary Pinckney, nicknamed "Pink" and "Willie," on April 24, 1857; and Lillie Blanche on January 10, 1859. In 1852, the family mourned the death of Vivian Burke Rose, who had not yet turned seven when she succumbed to a fever.

Life at Forest Grove must have been idyllic for Victor, with all the trappings of affluence about him and an excellent education courtesy of his father. He had many siblings around him, but they were apparently not as bookish as Victor. He was never adept at the rough and tumble games that were so much a part of his siblings' lives. Stories indicate that he was often the subject of ridicule when he attempted to join in outdoor and plantation-related games and activities.

Victor's sister Zilpa would often relay the story that when he was about twelve years old, he shot a sandhill crane and only injured it, in front of the Rose plantation home. Instead of running away, the crane turned on Victor and chased him into the house. He barely made it through the door in time to dodge the angry bird. This was much to the delight of his younger brothers and sisters.[41]

In her biographical sketch of Victor Rose, his niece, Kathryn Stoner O'Connor, says that although he could ride a horse—a necessity for getting from one place to another in those days—he was unlike most other Texas boys in that he could "could hardly tell one horse from another.... When attending parties and balls, his friends always had to find his horse for him after the parties, or he would be likely to mount the first horse he came to—one animal looked like another to him."[42]

His ignorance about farm and ranch life would extend even into adulthood. While staying at a brother-in-law's ranch and helping feed the livestock, he suddenly shouted, "Something is the matter with 'Bully'! He has become quite obstreperous." Victor had mistaken a wild yearling for the ranch's pet bull.[43] It would have to be assumed that the Rose family would prefer young Victor to stay inside with his books, rather than wreak havoc by attempting to engage in plantation activities.

Forest Grove continued to grow. Initially Judge Rose raised cattle and horses and cultivated crops such as corn and wheat, but by 1857, with the world demand for cotton products booming, he sold his stock and planted two hundred acres in cotton.[44] He also built a gin and a grinding stone, one of the oldest on the Guadalupe.[45] Zilpa would later recall that her father had "the finest yard in the county," because he ordered plants and trees from commercial nurseries.[46] The family lived in a large thirteen-room house, separated from the slave quarters by a brick path lined with pink and white periwinkles.[47]

Victor was apparently close to the family slaves in his youth. His ongoing relationships with the Rose family slaves and his proximity to the truth of what it was like to live in bondage likely influenced his strong antislavery stance later in life. One would have to wonder how many conversations took place between Victor and the family slaves, giving him insight into the abomination of slavery.

With the shift to cotton, Rose bought many additional slaves, adding to the original group that the Roses had been given upon their marriage, likely as wedding gifts, as was customary in the antebellum South. John

Rose's parents, William Pinckney Rose and Mary Vardeman Smith Rose, gave their son two men and three women—"Uncle Moses" and "Aunt Patience," a woman simply known to the children as "Mammy," and two individuals whose names are unknown. Margaret Rose's mother, Kate Keller Scott, gave her daughter "Uncle Peter" and "Aunt Eliza" and another couple whose names are lost.[48]

Then, in 1840, perhaps anticipating the extra labor involved in moving from Shelby County and setting up his own household in Victoria County, John Rose purchased two young slaves from his father-in-law, Samuel T. Scott: ten-year-old Henry Clay, later called "Big Henry" by the Rose children, and six-year-old Solomon. The purchase price was $1,050.[49] By 1860, Rose owned forty-eight slaves, valued at $30,000 in the county tax rolls.[50]

By about 1859, Judge Rose had put Victor and his brother Volney to work in Wheeler's general store, the largest in Victoria. Jesse O. Wheeler was one of Victoria's earliest settlers, a merchant and entrepreneur, and one of the county's five wealthiest men on the eve of the Civil War. He and his family would continue to play a role in the affairs of the Rose family in the years ahead.[51] There was to be a lifelong connection between the two families—not all of it friendly.

Wheeler sold not only groceries and a vast array of dry goods, which he advertised as "purchased and carefully selected by himself in New York, expressly for this market," but also clothing, shoes, saddlery, carriages, hardware, farm implements, stationery, perfumes, jewelry, wine and spirits, and "an immense number of other articles too tedious to enumerate."[52]

As Wheeler was engaged in other kinds of business transactions—such as loaning money and buying and selling livestock and cotton, the store was a hub of commerce where Victor interacted with a constant stream of townspeople and absorbed much local lore. He also lived in the Wheeler household for a time, as revealed in the 1860 census. These connections gave him a familiarity with Victoria that would serve him well when he later wrote of the town's history.

As a youth, he developed a reputation for "always getting into scrapes." Adolescence was a time of great tumult in Victor's life. His negative behaviors increased at an alarming rate in his teenage years. Unfortunately, this dysfunction and a tendency toward violence continued for much of his life. These behaviors particularly increased after the war and with heavy drinking.[53]

According to family accounts, while Victor was clerking at Wheeler's store, he got into trouble on Election Day in 1859. Most of the men in town had been drinking, and a brawl erupted in front of the store. Victor's brother Volney was knocked to the ground by a man known as "the Dutchman." Seventeen-year-old Victor rushed out to rescue Volney and, seeing the man holding his brother down and beating him, fired a pistol at the man and inflicted a wound.

They sent Victor back home, nine miles from town, so that he would not be put in jail. The sheriff came to the house, but he was a friend of the family and evidently did not pursue the matter. The man's family was finally satisfied when Judge Rose paid $500 as reparation.[54] Kathryn Stoner O'Connor recalls: "At 12 o'clock that night my father sent Jim Minor, Victor's brother-in-law to take Victor off and put him at school. They went in a carriage with a Negro driver to Indianola and then took a steamer for New Orleans. From there he was taken to Centenary College, where he was when the Civil War broke out. He joined the 3rd Texas Cavalry and was sent across the Mississippi River. A note in the family papers reads, 'Poor boy, he was always getting in trouble all his life.'"[55]

A more serious offense occurred the next summer. On June 25, 1860, a man known as "French Finger" filed a sworn statement with the justice of the peace charging that he had been assaulted by Victor the previous evening. He claimed that he had been visiting the house of a Mr. Voit when Victor, accompanied by an individual named Charles T. Wilson and another man, stood outside the house and demanded beer. According to Finger's statement, "Victor Rose said if they did not give him beer that he would kill everybody inside of the house."

Mrs. Voit then came to the door and told the three to go away, that this was not a "publick house," and that they "had no beer for other persons." Finger concluded his statement with the charge that Victor "shot at me and then he was caugh[t] by another man to keep him from shooting [anymore] and then I took the five shooter out of his hand."[56] Victor immediately posted a $500 surety bond. His sureties were Jesse O. Wheeler, his employer, and W. T. Mitchell, a longtime employee of Wheeler's. In August a grand jury indicted both Victor and Charles Wilson on the assault charge.[57] In Victor's day, especially in small communities, people and law enforcement would often overlook the "boys will be boys" behavior of prominent citizens, as we can see in several of Victor's capers.

According to family lore, Victor was hustled off to college after the fight with the so-called Dutchman, but it is much more likely that he left Victoria after the Finger incident led to an indictment.

When Victor arrived on Centenary's hundred-acre campus, he attended classes in the newly constructed Center Building, the largest structure devoted to education in the entire state of Louisiana. The building housed all classrooms, a large recitation room, an auditorium, a gymnasium, and the dining hall, chapel, and library. Two wings flanking the building contained dormitory rooms, each with its own fireplace. In the antebellum era, most students at the all-male college were the sons of planters and well-to-do merchants from the Deep South. Yet college life was Spartan and rigorous. The school day began at dawn and lasted until 9:00 p.m. Alcohol, dueling, and card games were not allowed, on or off campus.[58] Apparently, Victor's father had found the right place to send an errant son, so early in trouble and in need of taming.

At the age of seventeen, Victor was enrolled as a new student for the fall term of 1859, which began on October 1.[59] Admission to the freshman class required a knowledge of English grammar, geography, arithmetic, algebra, "Andrew's and Stoddard's *Latin Grammar and Reader*, Andrew[s]'s *Latin Lessons*, Caesar (four books), Brooks's *Ovid*, Cicero's *Orations*, Bullion's *Greek Grammar*, and *Bullion's Greek Reader*." The first-year curriculum consisted of Xenophon's *Anabasis*, the Greek testament, Virgil, algebra, classical geography, Livy, geometry, practice in Latin translation, and declamation and composition.[60] Notably, in the period before the outbreak of war, debates and other programs at Centenary did not address sectional issues. Students were focused on philosophical subjects such as "The Poet's Mission" and "The Upright Politician."[61] Victor must have been quite familiar with the curriculum, having spent his earlier years studying these works with his father. His formal education at Centenary undoubtedly contributed to the flowery nature of his writing and the classical references contained therein.

Upon his return from Centenary, surely Victor must have felt out of place among his peers and siblings at home, as well as with many of the adults in his life. Almost no one had the level of education he had received as a youth, possibly making him somewhat of an outcast. He likely felt more at home in an atmosphere of learning.

Up until this point in his life, Victor had been raised in a setting of privilege and protection that prepared him for nothing but these same fortunate circumstances in adulthood. Yet all of this was soon to change.

CHAPTER TWO

The Lost Cause and the Honor System of the South

1861–1865

§

"War is a cruel leveler, but time brings compensation."

—Letter from Victor M. Rose to
Col. John Henry Brown, February 17, 1889

BEFORE the Civil War, the gentry experienced a prosperous time with much leisure, often dedicating their time to politics. Planters sold cotton to buy more slaves to plant more cotton. Consumers spent heavily on merchandise from the North. Stockmen increased their herds, and bought unimproved lands with a view to their increase in value. It was a transition period when the old was reluctantly yielding to the new. It was a time of "aristocratic assumption" and "democratic simplicity." These two factors generated the prevailing influence, social as well as political, throughout the South.[1]

The stepping stones to the Civil War were falling in place. Exuberance swept over the South with the secessionist movement. Many supported secession but dreaded the inevitable conflict. This was Victor Rose, who, as did many, went along with the hysteria and momentum of the rebellion.[2]

Victor describes the times prior to the secession and war with a flowery version of slavery: "The Patriarchal simplicity of which, adorned by the glamour of sylvan romance—the half redeems the picture from the background of Negro slavery. Indeed the mutual confidence, and affection which subsisted between master and slave will in future times seem incredible to those not able to draw their deduction immediately from the source itself; for in all times to come there will be nothing in developed human nature analogous to it."[3]

Storm clouds were appearing on the horizon. Lincoln had been elected president and was in total opposition to all Southern philosophies and principles. In his writings, Victor declared Lincoln's election as the first step to war. The South began to rumble about secession, and Lincoln considered that a declaration of war. He was, as seen, the better of the Civil War leaders.

The Texas Ordinance of Secession was the document that officially separated Texas from the United States in 1861. It was adopted by the Secession Convention on February 1 of that year, by a vote of 166 to 8.[4] The adoption of the ordinance was one of a series of events that led to Texas' entry into the Confederacy and the American Civil War.[5]

Dissenters (i.e., those not for secession) were seriously scorned and ostracized by Southerners. They were called "scalawags."[6] Much of the dissent was based in opposition to slavery and was especially strong in the German communities.[7] Many dissenters were also pro-Union, and there was even a Southern Unionist movement.[8] Even Texas governor Sam Houston refused to take the oath of allegiance to the Confederacy. He agreed with states' rights, but warned the South that total devastation was on the way from the mighty North.[9] He never wavered from this opinion, and how right he was.

Author J. V. Ridgely stated that there was unanimity of sentiment throughout the South.[10] However, this proved not to be true, as there were many dissenters. Given his stance against slavery, Victor was probably a dissenter in his heart, but being Southern was a spiritual condition,[11] a sense of identity and self-consciousness. He apparently disagreed with secession, but the stigma and ostracism associated with not joining the Confederacy caused him to join, possibly against his better judgment. His later writings show that indeed he saw through the "Lost Cause" and the martyrdom mentality.

Even as war hysteria began, Victor's writings indicate that he knew slavery was wrong, but the racism in society as a whole was so pervasive he could not overcome abiding by the rules and mores of society. The South had an institution that would bring economic devastation if lost.

Being sharply distinguished from Northerners, as we have seen, Southerners relied heavily on sociability and honor. Thus, in Southern culture, without acceptance by one's social group, there was no happiness. One had to be a member of an honor group, and Victor appears to have decided to make the Confederate Army his. He was unable to go against the culture and honor code of the South. It had been ingrained in him from birth, and regrettably he joined in the frenzy, even to going to war and suffering serious injury, trauma, and the horrors of being a prisoner of war.

Victor's choice to join the Confederacy and go to war is perfectly explained in a letter to his parents when he left Centenary College to join the Confederate Army:

Dear Ma,   May 20th, 1861

Months long and weary months have slowly passed by causing much uneasiness on my part—without bringing from home a single line. Patiently did I await an answer of the many letters written you asking advice but alas no letter comes. As College is broken up it is folly to remain in Jackson idle. So after pondering long and carefully in my own mind and consulting the president as to what I should do, I have concluded and with his approbation for many reasons to leave. Hence I will leave tonight for Harrison Co.

Ma I hope that Pa and yourself will not become angry with this proceeding. It is no wild harumscarum move but the result of deliberate calm thought. Every body here belongs to a millitary [sic] company. Even the ladies have organized themselves into armed bodies for home protection. Some Young Gentlemen who were not going to the war were presented with a hoop Skirt each by the Young ladies.

Never upon this earth will such a thing hap[p]en to Victor Rose. No. Ma, I admit this is rather one of the extreme cases. But if I were to remain inactive during the war, I could never return home and be the same boy any way.

The gnawing canker would be buisy [sic] in my bosom and burning shame would set its indelible signet upon my brow.

Hoping what I have done will meet with your and Pa's approval I remain

Your affectionate and obedient Son

Victor

P.S. Give my love to all, tell the children howdy   VR[12]

This poignant letter shows Victor's sense of being isolated from the family and having to make his own decisions. Only one of three letters uncovered from Victor's college days, we have to wonder whether his previous letters to his parents asking for advice had gone unanswered because they felt he had disgraced the family and deserved to be left to his own devices in making his way in the world. The letter reveals Victor's worries about being regarded as a coward. The "sissy" epithet may have left its mark, and it cast doubt on the claim that he was "full of enthusiasm for the Cause," as his niece would later write.[13] He was also anxious about being blamed for taking such a rash action. This was "no wild harumscarum move," he assures his parents.

As the letter shows, Victor was a poor speller and remained so throughout his life, often spelling difficult words flawlessly while seeming unable to master much simpler words. More significantly, in this youthful letter, distinct features of his epistolary style are already apparent. His correspondence is filled with allusions, metaphors, and other figurative devices as well as lofty rhetoric, such as "indelible signet upon my brow"—all indicating that literary composition was a natural mode of expression for Victor, even when writing a basic letter to his family.

Victor had one peculiarity—he could not spell the little word "few" right. He would always misspell it "fiew." Of course, he knew better. It was only habit. Once during the Civil War, his father received a letter from Victor while he was a prisoner at Camp Chase. Some thought the letter was a forgery, as he was requesting so much, but his father was able to verify the authenticity of the letter by the errant spelling of "fiew." In family papers, Victor's younger sibling recounts, "I do not remember much of his longhand as I was 10 years old. . . . I was old enough to remember he was almost a man—he was always peculiar—went off alone, hunting and fishing he would walk miles did not like to ride."[14]

Victor's letter from Centenary is proof positive that he was not willing to face the humiliation he would suffer if he didn't serve in the Confederate military. It is also an explanation for why he changed his opinions so soon and so drastically after the war, showing the level of abject frenzy that had overtaken the South. Almost all of the South had "drunk the Kool-Aid."[15] The honor system of the South was so deeply embedded in society and in Victor's mind that it forced him to join in a dubious war and cause.

Had he remained in Jackson, he could not have continued his studies, regardless of the circumstances. Centenary College officially closed the following October when an anonymous hand recorded these famous words in the faculty minutes: "Students have all gone to war. College suspended; and God help the right!"[16] And with this, Victor went to war.

After leaving the scholastic world of Centenary College in May 1861, Victor entered the brutal fields of battle. His Civil War experiences not only forced maturity upon the young man but also gave him a sense of purpose and self-worth. As he would later write, in joining the Confederate Army, he was "a friendless wanderer . . . [who] cast his fortunes with them, and—call them rebels and traitors, revile the cause of the South as much as you will—he is prouder of his course, during those four years, than of any other period of his life."[17] This shows how he finally felt some sense of belonging in spite of the dangers he faced. His military career also served as proof that he was strong and not a "sissy."

Most of the students at Centenary were Louisiana natives, and most enlisted at Camp Moore, located at nearby Tangipahoa.[18] Although they joined Louisiana regiments that probably never crossed paths with Victor's regiment, he later pays tribute to several of the fallen Centenary students in his 1886 poem "Celeste Valcœur." Remarkably, although they were upperclassmen when he was a freshman, he was aware of their deaths, which may indicate that he made some enduring friendships at the college and corresponded with old classmates after the war ended.[19]

Victor had a very hard time in the Civil War, having joined Company A of the 3rd Texas Cavalry, known as "The Texas Hunters," under Col. Elkanah Greer. The regiment was soon after attached to Ben McCulloch's command and later to Ross's Texas Brigade. Having observed the horrors of war and then experiencing the even more horrific fate of the wounded, Victor emerged from the battlefield deeply scarred and emotionally wounded. In his only surviving letter from the war years, he mentions the widespread illness among the troops and expresses his relief at his own good health:

Camp Elission [Elysian?]   October 31st 1861

Dear Ma

I seat myself this evening to drop you a few lines to let you know that I am still enjoying health, notwithstanding the many cases of fever, pneumonia and measles now in our Regiment. I do not see for the life of me how I have avoided them all, for scarsely [sic] a single member of any company have been so lucky as they have all been sick. I never was as healthy in my life before. In fact camping life suits me better than any other. And I would be content to ever remain a soldier and seek the feeble fame or die and be claimed by oblivion as her own, but for the thoughts of <u>home</u>. When the noise of camp gives place to the quiet shades of night, I wander back in imagination to the scenes that lit up my boyish fancy. All the years of my childhood are lived over again. Scarsely an evening passes but I form one of the circle that draws around the fire with the ap[p]roaching shades of night. There is a charm associated with the name of home which distance cannot weaken or time efface.

There has been considerable movements here on the part of both Armies which I think will result in a pitched battle.

Fremont with 25,000 men and 40 pieces of can[n]on is encamped ten miles south of Springfield on the old battle ground. Price with his Missourians 35,000 are going to offer battle. McCulloch says he will not budge an inch, which I think is very wise in him. For Price is strong enough to dislodge him without our assistance. And should he fail, why we could trot there a happy string before they could enter Arkansas!

I think our Regiment will be furloughed and return home to spend the winter in less time than three weeks. It is well founded too. We will remain however until the coming fight is ended. Fremont is very cautious & makes his movements with great precision, not a flaw can be detected. He says he can whip us if we fight in open field, but that it would be impossible to drive us out of the hills and bushes where we are now stationed. And rest assured he will never get a chance at us in the open field, then ac[c]ording to his own admission we will be victorious.

It is rumored in camp that there has been another fight at Bull Run (Dutch Run) which oc[c]asioned great rejoicing in our camp. I understand that a letter has been found or intercepted from a Major in Fremont's Army to his wife. He says this will be their last contest for Missouri and it will be a desperate effort. The Legislature convened a few days ago and passed the secession ordinance. It is to be ratified by the people. I think they will carry it by a small majority or probably lose it as the greater portion of the state is oc[c]upied by federal troops.

As I can think of nothing more I will close.

Give my love to all and accept the portion due.

I remain your affectionate son

Victor.

N.B. I saw Hence Pregeon [Pridgen] the other day and I tell you I was glad to see him, but was disap[p]ointed in not getting some letters. I have received but one letter from home since I have enlisted. Direct your letters to Fayetteville, Ark.   VMR[20]

In this letter, again we see Victor steeped in the culture of power, pride, and prestige, along with the overall climate of anger and frustration that culminated in secession. His enlistment appears to be less about honor than a lack of courage at this time in his life to go against society's rules. There were also very little prospects for him at the outbreak of the war.

The letter indicates that Victor had fond memories of home and a happy childhood, even if his parents did not write to him as often as he would have liked. This letter home from war is probably the best insight we have into the real Victor Marion Rose.

Having been somewhat of a misfit most of his life, we can understand how Victor must have felt when he suddenly had a sense of purpose in life, surrounded by others who shared in the same mission. Considering what he went through in the war, it is hard to believe he was able to survive, having never been faced with physical hardship. However, the war may have taken its toll on Victor in a different form, as his war experiences and injuries may very well have contributed to his dependence on alcohol. We can only surmise this, but his behavior certainly followed a known pattern shared by those damaged by war.

Ross's Texas Brigade was formed in Dallas, Texas, in the first year of the war, and moved northward through Indian territory into northern Arkansas and southwestern Missouri. It also made an expedition back into the Indian country before marching down the Arkansas River to Little Rock and on to Duvall's Bluff on the White River, where it embarked for Memphis, down the White and up the Mississippi. It continued to Corinth and for the next year or more operated in Tennessee and northern Mississippi. In the spring of 1864, the brigade was with General Joseph E. Johnston on his retreat southward toward Atlanta. After the fall of that city, it followed General Hood[21] across Alabama and back through middle Tennessee to the outskirts of Nashville, where it participated in the battles that practically destroyed the Confederate Army.

Even in the mid-twentieth century, we see Victor's writings used as primary source material for other scholarly works on this subject. His experiences under Ross also provided the foundation for one of his most important works: *Ross' Texas Brigade: Being a Narrative of Events Connected with Its Service in the Late War between the States*. It was published twenty years after Victor joined the regiment that became known as Ross's Texas Brigade. The book contains his firsthand account of the war—and provides the only detailed record of his whereabouts and activities between 1861 and 1864. He ended the book with "The Lost Cause whose sun has set forever."[22]

He strongly praises Southern women who with dread and forebodings sent their men to war and shed bitter tears over the losses and defeats, referring to them as "angels, a peerless sisterhood, to be enshrined and put on a pedestal." He reasons that because these Southern women of such merit upheld the South, it could never be considered a "bad cause." Yet, this undying loyalty, Victor notes, could not save the South.

In his writings, Victor creates a colorful picture of events and activities in the time leading up to and surrounding the Civil War. He felt the South was left no alternative but to rebel, and this may have been another reason why he joined the Confederacy. He described the acceleration of war on both sides until it could not be stopped and the lines of demarcation were drawn. He notes that Southerners followed their hearts and principles, just as the Unionists, where the South probably knew in their hearts they could not win. Victor lauds this loyalty. Here we see emotion overtake reason with Victor, as it did with so many others.

As often occurs, he states how the youth and the "parlor knight" joined in the fray. He provides details that were all around him, from the corner store generals to those who smuggled cotton to the Yankees. These "Monday morning quarterbacks" were on every street corner. So off he goes to war, also thinking it wouldn't last a year, while soon he was re-enlisted until the war would end.[23]

He writes how Confederate soldiers were welcomed everywhere and how many connected with young women they might possibly reconnect with when the war was over. He also lamented that so many would not come back. He continues relating to the pathetic and inferior state of the South to the conditions in the North.

Victor makes a very interesting comment about Texas in particular.[24] He notes the ongoing bravery of Texas soldiers, and how Texas was their true nation—the only one they truly owed allegiance. He says Texas was allied with the rest of the Confederacy, but was not indissolubly joined. He also notes that the Indian tribes that joined with the Confederacy brought about their own ruin—even though they rallied behind the Confederacy and the cause of the South and fought bravely alongside the Texans, the Indians were not behind their Texan compatriots and were rather inhospitable to the men of the regiment.[25]

Victor goes on to state his case that secession was forced on the Confederacy and that it was an "extreme remedy," a "Caesarian remedy," "so radical in nature as to be resorted to only in the extremist case." He believed the only hope of the Confederacy was to engage in an aggressive warfare, a task in which they failed, remaining inefficient while their statesmen split "theoretical hairs."[26]

The poem "A Narrative of the Services of Ross' Texas Brigade of Cavalry, in the Late War between the States," by Victor, begins with the word "Rebellion!" He describes it as a foul and dishonoring word. Then he indicates that the stance of the South was not rebellion but defense of a noble cause. He notes that Lincoln was elected by a party with no other purpose but antagonism to the South and her most cherished principles and institutions.[27] However, this poem seems to echo popular sentiment rather than Victor's own beliefs about Lincoln in particular.

The third section of Rose's *History of Victoria County*, covering 1861 to 1865, begins with his description of the war fever that swept their region. While his account sounds somewhat breezy and celebratory, the prose turns somber and more thoughtful after the first paragraphs:

"Confederate flags fluttered in the breezes on every hand—and Folly was toppling a great State into needless, ruinous, rebellion. We repudiated the counsels of Sam Houston, Jack Hamilton, J.W. Throckmorton; John Hancock, and other Texans, to follow the magpie chattering of South Carolina's pigmy so-called statesmen. Had our embryo warriors been asked for what purpose they were going to war, doubtless the only reply in many instances would have been: 'To whip the Yankees!'"[28] Victor, throughout his works, seems to realize the futility if not downright stupidity of the pro-secession stance. He does concede that slave holders were at the basis of the final rebellion.[29]

This is a very important statement by Victor: "These people had no grievances of which to complain. They had known the federal government only as a fostering parent, and yet, they were enthusiastic for war against the old Union, as if years of oppression had driven them to the stern necessity. There was never a more causeless war."[30] This apparently the first inkling of his monumental change in attitude.

Then came the fall of Fort Sumter and the secession of Texas. Daily life and war activities were described thusly:

"Dixie" and "Bonnie Blue Flag" were heard on every tongue. Young men prepared for war, and whipping the Yankees was the daily chat-

ter. Young ladies engaged their silken hours of ease in making secession rosettes for their warlike cavaliers. They were engaged before a
great while in weaving "homespun" to take the place of threadbare
Yankee calico dresses. Confederate flags fluttered in the breezes on
every hand, and folly was toppling a great state into needless, ruinous,
rebellion. . . .

The fires of patriotism were burning in every bosom, and nothing
but war was thought of, and there was a general disposition to ignore
the deprivation of luxuries, and comforts to which they were reduced.
Thus in the journals of the day many substitutes were recommended
for coffee, some of which it was claimed were superior to the genuine
article. One editor seems to have become infatuated with "shoe black-
ing made of China berries," claiming that its gloss was far more perfect than the Yankee composition. But our credulity is severely taxed
by an enthusiastic gentleman of DeWitt County, who gives a recipe
for the manufacture of tallow candles "which are the equal of those
made of sperm." . . .

A patriotism that induces a people that have been always the pos-
sessors of comforts, and even luxuries, to regard a deprivation of such
as blessings in disguise, must certainly have been the genuine, Bunker
Hill article![31]

Take notice that Victor's understanding of the deadly and impossible
stance of the South appears all throughout his work. It has been sug-
gested that Victor did not approve of secession or at least understood
the dire implications of the whole thing. Certain accounts of family history appear to have ignored that fact, and declared he was enthusiasti-
cally pro-secession. However, it is quite possible that he merely engaged
in "go along" to "get along," and soon recovered from his delusionary state.

Here he notes that he does not think much of the leadership of the
Confederacy.[32] He draws painful visuals of the dying and wounded that
are truly upsetting.[33] He states that some of the things he witnessed
"[have] remained stamped on my mind as vividly as on that August
in 1861—known as flashbacks to modern medicine. He also believed
that the South was just destined not to win. While the troops' winter
encampments presented an opportunity for an active social life, all this
gaiety was to end soon as the enemy advanced.

Victor suffered greatly for and in sympathy with the victims of war—the Indians, the women and children, the blacks. He laments the ill fate of Indians who enlisted for the cause, only to play the role of cannon fodder for a cause that they had no way of understanding. His writings posit that death at times is preferable to living with the burdens of life and progressively show his loss of enthusiasm as the South fades into despondency.

Throughout the narrative, Victor constantly relays his admiration for leaders on the battlefields, and laments the ill fate of those who suffered at great cost. *Ross' Texas Brigade* tells the tale of B. P. Simmons, with half the calf of his left leg shot away in battle. After his ordeal, Simmons was taken to the hospital, where he was placed on a blanket between two soldiers, Goodson King and Spearman, both belonging to Company D, 6th Texas, and both with their legs shattered by grape shot. King died that night, and Spearman the next morning. "This is an incident that we read of in the exploits of ideal heroes in romances; how seldom do we ever come upon the incident verified, as in this instance?"[34]

In the heat of war, Victor notes that the brigade was sent to unexpected places, and one gets the feeling that a chaotic situation was at hand. We also see his unending efforts to vigorously research all aspects of the war, and to diligently search for documentation relating to his writings. He also writes about "peerless ladies," and the brigade's strict orders not to dare harm any women they encountered. He often injects humor[35] into his most serious writings, and posits that this admiration of women caused soldiers on both sides to refrain from the total destruction of towns.

In *Ross' Texas Brigade*, Col. John Griffith addresses his soldiers: "Men, offer no rudeness to the ladies; if they will not allow you to pass through the gate, tear off a picket from the fence, and flank them; if you are denied admittance at the door, go around them, and find ingress through a window. You must search the house for concealed prisoners, but do not touch the hem of the garment of one of these ladies."[36]

Victor had the ability to draw colorful pictures of situations he had seen personally or collected from others.[37] He connects real events in his life to the idealized heroes in romances,[38] no doubt instilled in his mind throughout his early life and formal education. He had a talent for connecting historical events to classic literature.

He describes the Civil War as a "tragic drama."[39] In his description of one of the battles, he says, "the sun set as if ashamed to witness the scene of slaughter."[40] Throughout his writings, we see compassion in Victor and more and more trauma being inflicted upon him, which undoubtedly contributed to his increased drinking and violent lifestyle after the war. On the battlefield, he laments, "The guns of the enemy thundered their vomiting of iron hail into the decimated ranks of the Texans."[41] He was tireless in his compilation of firsthand information, testimonials, and personal diaries, referring to these experiences as "that galaxy of glorious stars."[42] In his *Travels in the Confederate States*, Dr. E. M. Coulter, eminent historian of the Confederacy, indicates, "Victor Rose's statements about Confederates capturing and pillaging the Federal supplies in Holly Springs, Mississippi, are frank and graphic." [43] Victor provided any and every detail possible, becoming an invaluable source of information for modern scholars researching the truth about this tumultuous time in American history.

Back home, the Rose plantation started to feel the effects of the Civil War as early as July 1861 with the federal blockade of Galveston, the state's major port and the gateway of commerce for Victoria County. Supplies coming from New Orleans and New York via Galveston were cut off, and cotton shipments from Texas could no longer reach the lucrative markets of Liverpool.

Plantations like Forest Grove had difficulty finding buyers for their cotton, which had to be sent by way of Mexico and then on to Europe. Smuggling by blockade runners became rampant. More food crops were grown, especially with meat and staples being diverted to feed soldiers. Tea, spices, and coffee were now luxury items, and many newspapers printed advice on ways to concoct substitutes for coffee: "Rye scorched, or the acorns of a species of white oak tree very common in Mississippi and the Gulf States, is a good substitute for coffee. . . . The okra seeds also make a tolerable substitute for coffee."[44]

Victor's sister, Zilpa, recalled that the family's groceries and dry goods came from Mexico during the war and that the women, white as well as black, made clothes for the soldiers: "As the war grew, we all who were old enough spun and knit for the soldiers. . . . We also . . . knit sox and scarfs and sweaters.[45] In February 1863, on a trip to Victoria to collect hand-sewn uniforms for the troops, Volney Rose placed the following notice in the *Victoria Advocate*:

> To the patriotic ladies:
>   The material which has been so anxiously and long looked for has at last arrived—at least a portion of it—and the remainder will be here before this can be made up. Mr. Karn, tailor, will commence at once to cut the garments and myself and Mr. J.R. Crew will be here to deliver them at the old J. Roselle store on Main street next Monday.
>   V.J. Rose, 2nd. Sergt. 4th Texas Cavalry

The *Advocate* editor added, "We have no doubt but many of our brave friends are in want of these garments and we hope our fair friends will be prompt in the labor of love and patriotism."[46] As Civil War historians have noted, the Confederacy was unable to supply its soldiers with enough uniforms and relied on women's sewing circles and relief societies to provide clothing and other provisions.[47]

Along with the adjustments to life during wartime came sorrows. The Rose children's sixty-five-year-old slave "Mammy" (Manerva Warrior) died in 1864, while holding a picture of Victor, and was buried in the family cemetery at Forest Grove. "We all loved [her] more than our Mother," said Zilpa, "for she took the care of us. We went to her with all our childish troubles."[48]

Victor's combat service ended abruptly during the Atlanta campaign at the Battle of Lovejoy Station on August 20, 1864.[49] He had previously been wounded three times, once seriously, taking a bullet in the head. He was later captured and imprisoned in the notorious Camp Chase in Ohio, where he nearly starved to death as a prisoner of war.

Victor tells of being captured by Brig. Gen. Judson Kilpatrick and of the exhausting march he and his fellow solders were subjected to. They were in the saddle for three days with little to no food. It is noted by Victor that the Union troops were not much better off, but had the humanity to share what little they had with the Confederate prisoners, humanely treating the captured. Victor notes that the Union soldiers themselves were abused, described them as unfortunates, and noted that it was the "home guard" who misused them. He lamented the stance of politicians who refused to end the rancor and adopt the attitude of Gen. Ross—on the battlefield, they were all brethren.[50]

Only the soldiers who had confronted each other in battle seemed to understand each other's point of view and their enemies' great bravery, and had no wish to inflict more pain on each other. Victor also notes that most of the Confederate generals understood that it was a lost cause and that the Confederacy no longer existed. Only Jeff Davis and other "impractibles" imagined the Confederacy remained intact.

One would have to wonder at what point Victor accepted this harsh reality. Could it have been when he and his fellow prisoners arrived at Sherman's quarters? Here they were fed a meal of sow belly and hard tack. Victor was apparently quite repelled by what he met at the camp and described his encounters with "whining, canting, oath hypocrites and sycophants." The Confederate prisoners began extolling the superiority of the North and maligning all things Southern and Confederate. Perhaps their behavior was a farce aimed to achieve favors of food and comforts in light of their new hopeless situation. Regardless, Pvt. Crabtree could not brook this and began to defend the South. Victor provides a detailed account of what followed when a scuffle broke out among the newly converted prisoners and Crabtree. He interestingly and perceptively notes that the Unionists themselves despised these new converts, as most involved in the war hated those who deserted their own cause.[51]

Soon the prisoners were taken to Nashville, where they were locked in a prison for fear of being rescued by Gen. Wheeler, who was in the region with a large cavalry force. Then they were taken to Louisville by train, where all of their belongings were confiscated, never to be seen again. Through Cincinnati and Columbus, Victor and his fellow prisoners were taken to Camp Chase on the Scioto River in Ohio, where they were to spend the next nine months.

One must wonder how Victor managed to even stay alive on the trip to Ohio. He was not a physically strong person and suffered many injuries during the war, having been deprived of proper nutrition for quite some time. And yet he hung in and kept going.

He and his companions were carefully watched by numerous guards atop a fifteen foot wall. They slept in tiers of bunks where they were fed four ounces of white fish and three crackers daily. How any of them could survive this is cause for incredulity. Even when beef and flour was served, it was only in starvation-level quantities, leaving many to die.

Victor describes in detail how many men lost their self-respect and "the worst passions of our nation dominated over the good." We can only imagine what he saw and experienced in this situation. A few supplies were available, but nothing edible came in. Trading and a grocery business sprang up. Many starving prisoners would trade their food for tobacco products. Robberies began to happen, and punishment for this crime was very much akin to waterboarding. The rules of law often fell through the cracks, and terrible torture occurred in the camps. Many died from this, and others, some horribly wounded, lost their minds. Most simply walked aimlessly around the camp like caged animals.[52]

Victor tells of someone else from Victoria, John D. Miller, who was able to convey some "sutlers checks" to Victor from another camp. People were despairing and abandoning the Confederacy, and Victor, the "sissy," managed to survive on a daily basis in a deadly situation without becoming a traitor to his cause.

Through the winter and into spring, Victor hung on to life only to suffer the horrible news of Lincoln's assassination and Lee's surrender. Although there was no hope of victory left, surely Victor must have been at least secretly elated that the torture was over.[53] Victor realized just how detrimental the loss of Lincoln was for the South.[54]

The soldiers were reminded that they had lost the war but not their honor. They cheered this concept, and Victor and his group were sent by rail to New Orleans. Kind-hearted citizens helped them in Cairo, and passing through New Orleans they were sent to Vicksburg, where they were watched by a black guard. He continued to vacillate back and forth about slaves, slavery, blacks, and many aspects of this issue.[55]

Thus began the collective state of denial that followed the war, with each side claiming the other dealt out the most mistreatment. Victor reports that he and his fellow soldiers could not have been treated any worse and still survived. From Victor's accounts, as always, both sides were guilty of many crimes, and Victor leaves his readers and posterity to judge the matter. Later, we see his change of heart about his beloved South and its beliefs and practices.[56]

Released in 1865, he went to Vicksburg to recover from his war wounds.[57] How Victor survived his time at Camp Chase is hard to comprehend. The fact that he was quite young and came from the easy life of a wealthy plantation owner who was not accustomed to hardship made his survival all the more remarkable. He was wounded, and more than two thousand died at Camp Chase—but somehow Victor managed to survive.

During this time of transition, Victor was in close proximity to many of the notable persons of his time. Serving alongside Ross and the McCulloch brothers, he would later portray both men in their respective biographies. Victor's writing about his trip home is heartbreaking. When he was released after nine long months, he was so weak that he could hardly stand. On a Mississippi River steamer near Vicksburg, where he apparently recuperated, he saw a child eating an orange. He was strongly tempted to snatch it from the child and had to remove himself to the other end of the boat. This account of hunger and desperation is one of his most heartrending descriptions of the entire war.

Victor's recuperation took place on the Yellow River[58] at the home of a friend, Mr. Jackson. Here he was taken care of for nine months. He was so starved that soups, gruels, and milk were all he could eat for days. He was at this plantation from July 1865 to December 1865, when his father sent for him. It had been five years since he left home. Upon his return, he found only desolation and demoralization. Judge Rose was dying of tuberculosis, and the workers refused to work.[59] Victor and Volney Rose tried to farm but were unaccustomed to manual labor and failed. Northern "Yankee" occupation troops were stationed at Forest Grove and destroyed the orchards and animals. During Reconstruction the taxes on the plantation were so high that it was impossible for the family to pay them. Victor's childhood home, Forest Grove, was forever lost.[60]

Homeless and weary, Victor was deeply disturbed by his war experiences and began a life of restless geographical relocation. Considering what we know now about the psychological trauma of war, not to mention his physical wounds, it is amazing he was able to pick up his life and be productive at all. He quickly turned to drinking as a coping mechanism. The scars of war ran deep and were little understood at this time, with veterans given no resources or support.

The Rose and Stoner families all died martyrs to the "Cause." Nostalgia was rampant among them, as it was among all Southerners. It would be interesting to know if Victor engaged in arguments with his own family about these outdated attitudes.

Southerners were incomprehensible to others. The mentality, the pathos, martyrdom, consternation, doom, loss, and apocalypse left several generations broken and under assault by those not of the same mindset. In spite of all this, Victor came home and began a period of emotional and personal disruption, surely due to the destruction of the lifestyle that he was accustomed to and the serious damage he endured during the war.

Onward he goes in his writings, at times drawing from his deep knowledge of ancient history. He writes that the United States had won the war because they were the nation destined by God to disseminate liberty and that this gave the South no chance to win. Now the South should stand by the United States and its Constitution.[61] This is a remarkable line of thinking from someone so recently on the frontlines for an opposing cause, yet Victor, who saw this history as headed for oblivion, still remained deeply proud of his support of the South. He, to the end, adhered to the code of honor of the South, if not the institution of slavery.

CHAPTER THREE

A Wanderer's Return

1866–1869

VICTOR'S life changed greatly after the Civil War. He had to work, as did many Southern gentry—a necessity most found distasteful.[1] It was noted that even decades later, his nieces, Mame Stoner Stoner and Kathryn Stoner O'Connor, were ridiculed about their postwar poverty, so we can only imagine what Victor must have endured while trying to adjust to postwar conditions. He quite likely suffered ridicule about his newly impoverished condition.[2]

For a time, Victor appeared to be a lost soul, physically and emotionally wounded by war, untrained to work, and left without a visible means of support.[3] His habit of staying with relatives after the war was not unusual, as there were so many poverty-stricken people in the South. Margaret McLean put it quite plainly: "[P]eople just didn't have money."[4]

There is no doubt that life was wretched and miserable for the defeated Southerners, but they refused in many cases to change and make a life in their new and strange world. Because he did change and make his way in a changed world, Victor was seen as unusual to both outside observers as well as his own family. This alone makes him worthy of study. He had moved from the scholastic world into the brutal world of war and needed to adapt and evolve in order to survive.

In his *History of Victoria County*, Victor describes the disappearance of once-familiar scenes: "After an absence of five years the writer stepped into J. O Wheeler's store on Main street. In the commodious house there was absolutely nothing in abundance but space; and the long lines of shelves like skeletons grinning a welcome to the wanderer's return."[5] Federal troops in Texas had been discharged by this time, and most of the occupation forces of Reconstruction had been reduced,[6] but Forest Grove bore the mark of marauders who had destroyed fruit trees, crops, and poultry.

Victor was a man destined to inherit, but the Civil War destroyed that chance. A Southern gentleman of the landed gentry was almost useless after the Civil War. Most had never done real work in their lives. Victor is a good example of how a few of the educated gentry "got on with it" after the war. His education, while spanning back to ancient, classical times, did not prepare him for much but a literary pursuit. His written works show us, among other things, the lingering chivalry of the Old South, and how he was able to rise above this attitude and deal with the real world of Reconstruction.

Reconstruction was simply an extension of the war, during which most followed their designated or self-designated leaders, as they had during the war. The slave also went from being protected to being constantly disabused of any illusion that his liberty was real. Former slaves were now considered a danger to be held off with desperate measures if necessary. The bars came down with unprecedented completeness and fury. Thus emerged the Ku Klux Klan.[7] This time of transition pressed on, leaving the Old South changed forever.

"His four years of life in the Army, with its wild adventures and deeds of derring-do left [Victor] with a restlessness that kept him from settling down in one place for many months which kept him moving from one to another place and other occupations."[8] And there he was—beautifully educated and no way to make a living without a drastic change in his life, a person who had been a perfect example of the culture, lifestyles, and attitudes of the Old South. The gentry's overbearing and at times brutal approach to the outside world had to be laid aside as their aristocratic world came under siege.

Victor had a history of a violent nature throughout his life, especially when he consumed alcohol, which appeared to be more often than just socially, and there would be more "wild" behavior to come. As if acknowledging his impetuous nature, he would later adopt the pen name "Wild Rose" in some of his poetry. His wildness, rebellion, and lack of respect for the laws of society are apparent in his nom de plume.

Another cloud on the horizon was the stack of arrest warrants accumulating after Victor had failed to appear in court in his 1860 assault case. A capias[9] writ filed in September 1864 included a notation by the sheriff that neither Victor Rose nor Charles T. Wilson could be found in the county. But once Victor had returned home, the sheriff was able to execute the pending warrant, and on January 12, 1866, Victor was arrested. Accompanied by his father, he posted another bond—this one for $250. For unknown reasons, the case dragged on, with Victor posting another bond for $500 in December 1870. Finally, in 1871, case no. 370, *State of Texas vs. Victor M. Rose*, was quietly dismissed.[10]

Victor knew about the loss of the family plantation and really didn't care about it, oblivious to the work that needed to be done. He and his brother Volney did try their hand at farming but had no success. Forest Grove's time as a great plantation was over, having been confiscated by the Reconstruction forces at the end of the war. During this time Victor was socially ostracized, probably due to his advancing alcoholism, his sporadic aberrant relationships with women, and his newfound courage to go against the South.[11]

Victor was back home for a time after this, but was already aware he would have to make his own way in life. His father was despondent: there was no possibility of keeping the plantation going and Victor was no good at the rural and agricultural life anyway. Furthermore, Judge Rose was dying of tuberculosis as well as a broken spirit. In Zilpa's words, "My father was a secessionist. He never gave up that the South would win, until the surrender. Even then, he thought that the states west of the Mississippi could whip the Yankees. . . . My father was a staunch Rebel, and when he saw that we were whipped, he gave up. . . . He said he would not live under Yankee rule. But he got so despondent, that he gave up and said he would die."[12] The defeat of the Confederacy was such a crushing blow to Judge Rose, whose "hopes were all centered in the cause of the South," that he resolved to emigrate to Cordova, Mexico.

In a letter from 1883, Victor wrote, "My father and myself once set out for Mexico—1866—intending to leave the U.S., but were precluded by his wretched health from so doing. He never assimilated with the new order of things; and was himself no more after the 'Conquered Banner' was furled. The blow that toppled the Confederacy was fatal to him."[13]

While he understood the resentment that his fellow Southerners would long hold toward Yankees, Victor accepted the outcome of the "late upheaval" as a realist. Quoting Lincoln, he wrote, "We made a manly fight, and were whipped; and it was just as many to honestly recognize the fact, and accept the result. To repine, and upbraid fortune was but to 'plead the baby act;' and to nurse vindictive resolutions was to exchange the high precepts of civilization for the groveling code of the savage."[14] Even in his harshest criticisms of radical Reconstruction policies, Victor never wavered from his view that the war was a mistake. This statement alone shows a side of Victor that is remarkable for his time and place and as a Southerner.

A realistic attitude did not change the hard facts, however. The plantation economy of Victoria County was in shambles. Without the reliable supply of slave labor, cotton production slumped. Between 1860 and 1867, Texas lost 36 percent of its taxable wealth, and real estate in Victoria County declined an average of 70 percent, whereas the average decline in the rest of the state was 28 percent.[15] In the case of John Rose, county tax rolls show that Forest Grove's 4,428 acres were valued at $35,000 in 1860 but only $15,498 in 1867.

With the higher taxes that came with Reconstruction, many landowners were forced to sell or surrender their property at a loss. Although the Texas population was increasing due to waves of immigration and therefore more land was being put under cultivation, the average size of a farm had decreased. Victor ruefully summed up the situation this way:

A great many of the newly emancipated free men moved to town; agriculture languished, and all of the princely plantations of the olden time were shorn of their fair proportions. Small farms, it was soon demonstrated, was the only profitable scale upon which to court the favors of dame Nature. In this competition, based upon native merit, the thrift of the German farmer was soon made manifest. The American grumbled, cursed the Yankees, the drought, the high taxes, went into debt, and, in too many instances, finally sold out at a sacrifice, and sought cheaper lands, better Yankees, and a more propitious nature in the sparsely settled counties of the west.[16]

Some planters tried to keep their newly freed slaves as hired hands, but at Forest Grove the blacks stayed only a few months and then left. Zilpa remembered how one of the women cried when she said her good-byes, and all the Rose siblings cried, too. "Oh, how I loved the Negroes," said Zilpa. "They were all the friends and companions I had, until 1865, when they were freed.... We thought ourselves no better than our little black playmates."[17]

It was never really understood by many plantation and slave owners that regardless of their affinity for and fair treatment of the slaves, they were still humans owned in bondage like animals. Many slave owners were kind to their animals also.

At one point, Judge Rose must have tried to keep Forest Grove afloat by borrowing money, but he apparently defaulted on at least two loans. In March 1866, judgments were entered against him for debt on the two notes with interest rates of 8 and 12 percent, and he was ordered to pay the plaintiffs a total of more than $2,000.[18] Clearly the family could not raise this sum, and after her husband's death, Margaret Rose would be forced to begin the humiliating process of auctioning off property to settle the debts.

Despite the family's financial straits and Victor's legal troubles, the end of the war called for celebrations, and social life inevitably returned to normalcy. With the men home from the front, parties and dances resumed. According to Victor's niece:

In spite of the poverty and prostrate condition in which the "Break Up" left the South, plus the dangerous times of Reconstruction, our parents told us that the young people were never so gay nor had such good times. For four long years, the boys had been away in the army, and the girls sat at home and sewed. Now that the boys—some of them—were home again and avid for the company of girls, it was easy to get up dances, picnics and house parties without end. An old Negro fiddler and someone to call the figures was all that was necessary for an all-night dance. Square dances, the Lancers and schottische were the popular dances. Waltzes were considered too intimate, immoral. The girls wore calico or Tarleton dresses. The boys were in the remnants of their Confederate uniforms.[19]

During his wandering years after the Civil War, Victor, always known as a ladies' man, got into several bad situations with women. There were always hush-hush stories of Victor's peccadilloes and scandals. Kathryn Stoner O'Connor describes Victor in her biography as to his "susceptibility to the charms of ladies even when he was quite young."[20] His sister, Zilpa Rose Stoner, wrote in her memoirs: "Some of the girls Victor was in love with when he first returned home (from the war) were Nannie Stoner (his brother-in-law, G.O. Stoners' daughter) and Julia Hardy, whom he married."[21]

In the spring of 1866, Victor married Julia Holmes Hardy. Born about 1848 in Victoria, Julia was the daughter of Margaret Heffernan Dunbar Hardy and Milton Hardy, a prosperous rancher who had died of cholera in 1852. Several years later Margaret married her third husband, Alexander Borland, one of the wealthiest stockmen in Victoria County. Victor and Julia would have likely become acquainted at social events, as the Borlands and Roses moved in the same circles. A family guest list from 1865 in Zilpa's memoirs, for example, includes Margaret Borland and her family, and Zilpa mentions that the Roses had attended a dance and supper at the Borlands', who lived only nine miles from Forest Grove.[22] The fact that Victor wrote a love poem to Julia, likely in 1863, indicates that they had met before he left Victoria for college:

To Miss Julia Hardy

Lady! thy eyes are soft and bright,
Beaming holiest love;

Thy marble brow is wreathed with light,
Resplendant [*sic*] as above.
Thy classic lip would scorn to air
Hellen [*sic*], beauteous greek.
Aspiring Hebe would never dare
Surpass thy gentle cheek.

But great far beyond compare,
O Earth, or realms Above,
Surpassing all that's true or fair
Is my own matchless love.
Above, one star the less doth shine,
Since thou art here on earth.
Angels for thee methinks would pine—
Without thee bliss were dearth.[23]

Both families must have felt that Victor and Julia had married well.
Victor came from a prominent Victoria family, possessed charm and
wit, and had acquitted himself well in the war. Julia was the daughter
of a woman who kept an elegant home with a piano, walnut furniture,
marble-top bureau, and a full set of china.[24] She had a good education
and proper manners, and was "perfectly at home in the drawing rooms
of the cultured," as Victor would later describe his mother-in-law.[25]
Moreover, Julia had inherited property from the considerable estate of
her father, Milton Hardy. In the tax rolls of 1866, Julia and her sister,
Rosa, are listed as the owners of 934 acres of the old Navarro grant, with
their stepfather, Alex Borland, as guardian.

Unfortunately, Julia died of yellow fever shortly after the birth of her
daughter, Julia Rosa, in 1867. Yellow fever was raging at the time, and
a law was passed that victims had to be buried soon after death. Her
coffin was taken to the graveyard immediately, and Victor and a friend
stayed in the cemetery all night in case she may have only been in a
coma, as sometimes happened with yellow fever.[26] This was a loss from
which he never fully recovered.

Later in life he wrote a very lengthy poem to Julia, but penned this
shorter version soon after her death:

Poem to Dead Wife

Ah, Julia, there was an angle indeed;
The Star of my hope, my life.
I long for the bonds of earth to be freed,
And in Heaven you my wife.

Some might consider that Victor truly loved Julia, and had she lived,
he would he have led a different life, avoiding misbehavior and affairs
with women.

Victor also came close to death in the epidemic. He "who was also a
victim of the fever but whose life was saved, he felt, by the devoted care
and nursing of his friend and companion, Frank Pridham, who took his
bereaved friend to the Pridham home." Having returned home after his
wife's burial early the next morning, he almost immediately took sick
with yellow fever himself. He never seemed to have good health afterward.[27] Yellow fever and the ravages of war were to take a huge toll on
his health for the rest of his life.[28]

Dancing parties quickly resumed in Victoria after the war, and Rose
penned a verse that mimics the dialect and rhythm of an African American square dance caller (which was reprinted as "Jake's Quadrille" in
his 1886 collection of poetry, *While the Spell of Her Witchery Lingers*).
He also describes what he calls "the harmless craze of burlesque chivalry" and notes that Victoria's first "tournament," a social gathering was
held in 1868 after an order of knighthood was organized, designed to
celebrate the traditions of the Old South. "The first tournament in Victoria, so far as I have been able to determine, was held on August 19,
1869. I have an invitation to this tournament, which was addressed to
Miss Annie Wellington."[29]

Victor Rose was one of the main organizers of these gatherings and
also wrote most of the speeches and poems connected with them. His
writings at this time show his adherence to the myths of the Old South.

Margaret McLean recalls: "Uncle Vic [Rose] wrote all the speeches
for the ladies who accepted the honors at the tournaments. Aunt Kate
[Kathryn Stoner O'Connor] detailed all this to me, and my theme was

that it was a result of the Civil War. They had nothing to do when they came back. The whole land had just gone to ruin, you know. That's when the cattle drives started, because they didn't have anything. The people, for amusement, the Stoners, were heavily involved. All this was from the Scottish writer, Sir Walter Scott and his *Waverley Novels*."[30]

It was at this time that Victor turned to his pen to make a living. This was likely easier for him than some others, as he was never an adventurous outdoor type.[31] From an early age he was proficient at writing, which was his true talent, not an avocation, as it might have been if his life as a Southern gentleman hadn't been interrupted. He was luckier than most, who lacked talents other than their agrarian pursuits before the war. In 1869 Victor became the editor and publisher of the *Victoria Advocate*.

Victor had also become coeditor of the local weekly in October 1869, as announced by the October 23 issue of the *Galveston Daily News*: "Victor Rose has associated himself with Mr. James Boone in editing and publishing the *Victoria Advocate*." In February 1870 Victor's friend, Frank Pridham, replaced Boone. Only one issue of the *Victoria Advocate* from the period of Victor's tenure is known to be extant: the one of February 26, 1870, which is now in the newspaper collection of the Alamo Research Center in San Antonio.

The editorials in this issue target Reconstruction policies and the Radical Republicans, which had been instrumental in preventing former Confederate supporters from voting or holding office (a policy opposed by Lincoln before his death). At this time, Texas had not yet met the requirements for being readmitted to the Union, and Democrats like Rose felt that state government was in the hands of "mis-representatives of the people."

One editorial heaps scorn on William H. Parsons of Montgomery County, a former Confederate general who had joined the Republican Party and won election as a state senator in the provisional government, and was thus viewed by most Democrats as a scalawag—a Southerner who supported Reconstruction policies. Titled "Ex-Confederate General W.H. Parsons," the editorial was prompted by a speech in which Parsons attempted to explain his vote in favor of the Fifteenth Amendment to the Constitution, which had been ratified by the Texas legislature the previous week:

> This gentleman is a whale, in comparison to which, Jonah's famous fish was a sardine, judging from the amount of spouting he did on the occasion voting aye on the ratification of the Fifteenth Amendment. He arraigns the Northern Democracy for treason, and refers to the Charleston Convention and other fossil caucuses to bear him out, as if the situation was the same then as now. Not content with that, he wanders down the vistas of time and finds in tomes of roman lore, the very argument that is wanted to support the ratification of the Fifteenth Amendment; yet, he knows there is no similarity between the cases. He would make of the apostle Paul, a nigger to show that the Roman law recognized him as a citizen. He bleats aloud for universal suffrage as the only means by which the Government can be perpetuated, and votes for the Fifteenth Amendment for the consum[m]ation of that object, knowing that it secures the "barbarian ballot," holds in disfranchisement thousands of the best and ablest of his own race. The song is an old one, and had it come from other lips, would have awakened no surprise. Let the General speak, for the "day of his destiny" is short.[32]

Even at this early stage in his newspaper career, Rose hones his ability to skewer a politician with effective metaphorical language.

Another editorial is a dissection of a piece written by Ferdinand Flake, editor of *Flake's Bulletin*, a pro-Union, antislavery daily published in Galveston. In the gubernatorial election of 1869, Flake supported Andrew J. Hamilton, a Republican, against Edmund Davis, another Republican who won by a narrow victory. Rose suggests that Flake is attempting to heal the split between the two factions as a way of currying favor with the winning administration:

> Mr. Flake was one of the Captains who led them on to the civic battle. Surely his heart was in the movement; he could not have been influenced by the hope of public patronage. And now that the battle is lost, will he desert his followers simply because they can be of no more

service to him, and pass over to his political foe, because, forsooth, they are flushed with victory, and enjoying the spoils of office, and he seek absolution for the past, and hope to find in the Radical ranks the shortest road to public preferment.—Most seriously, if the *Bulletin* is a true exponent of the party it co-operated with in the late election, then were nine-tenths of its adherents misled; and had the "cloven foot" been thus exhibited before the election, the Conservative vote would have been but a corporal's guard. But we imagine Mr. Flake will see the hopelessness of his "peace" feeler and he himself again by the time his "ancient neighbor" gets back into the Democratic fold.[33]

On a lighter note, Rose corrects an error in a previous issue, in which he had mistakenly called the *Central Journal*, a Crockett newspaper, by the wrong name. The editor, R. R. Gilbert, pointed out the error: "The *Victoria Advocate* man calls our sheet the 'Centerville Journal.' Well, he is not the first man we have met whose education has been neglected. Try it again, Mr. Rose—Mr. Victor Rose." Here is Rose's amusing riposte: "Our mind was fuddled by reading High Private's articles on 'Gas.' We will desist in future and take kindly to Brick Pomeroy's 'Saturday Night' over which, to use the chaste and refined language of the *Central Journal*, *He slobbers over*. So."[34]

Other news items in this issue have the mark of Rose's characteristic humor, as in this description of the battered face ("phiz") of a coachman who claimed to have been attacked by ruffians in Galveston: "the poor fellow's probos[c]is was the size of a half grown watermelon." In another piece he describes the arrival of spring with poetic language that leads to a philosophical reflection on the similarity between spring and death: spring visits the rich and poor alike, just as "the slimy worm enters indifferently the wooden box of the pauper and the grand mausole[u]m of the Monarch."

By the summer, however, announcements had appeared in area newspapers that Victor was leaving the paper:

We regret to notice in the last number of the Victoria *Advocate* the valedictory of its senior editor, Mr. Victor M. Rose. Our retiring confrere has endeared himself to the fraternity for his courteous, dignified and able style of address, and won the lasting gratitude of the people for his undeviating and masterly advocacy of principle.

We hope, ere long, to see him connected with some leading Democratic press; for the country can illy spare the labors of one so eminently qualified to advance its political and material interests.

Mr. Pridham has become sole editor and proprietor, and will continue to make the *Advocate* worthy of an extended patronage.[35]

Victor continued to submit occasional pieces to the *Advocate*. One of the Austin papers, the *Tri-Weekly State Gazette* of December 25, 1871, reprinted a criticism of the state's legislators that had appeared in the *Advocate* and that sounds very much like Rose: "Nothing in the category of crime that these scoundrels could conspire, would surprise us. They are bomb-proof in their villainy—far beyond the pale of our anathemas, and in their turpitude, count the rewards of infamy, as the courtesan does the silver wages of sin." The same issue of the *Gazette* contained this intriguing comment: "The columns of the *Victoria Advocate* are embellished with racy historic sketches of the noted women of Europe, by Victor M. Rose, the accomplished sociate editor."

Thus we see Victor return from war, suffer a period of depression and posttraumatic stress disorder, marry, and have a child. He also held down jobs once he leveled out, but after the loss of his wife, he once again sinks into a time of depression and disorientation.

CHAPTER FOUR

Wild Rose

1870–1879

VICTOR'S departure from the *Advocate* in July 1870 may indicate that he was thinking of following in his father's footsteps by taking up a law career. According to a statewide legal directory compiled in the mid-1870s, he was admitted to the bar in August 1870 in Victoria,[1] but there is no evidence that he ever practiced law. By 1871, he reestablished his editor/publisher career with Frank R. Pridham at the *Advocate*.[2]

Whatever his plans, he must have been active in local Democratic politics, for in May 1872 he was officially informed that he had been elected Victoria County's delegate to the state Democratic Convention, to be held in Corsicana beginning on June 17.[3] The purpose of the convention, which Victor presumably attended, was to nominate national congressional candidates and presidential electors. Victor's interest in state politics would be lifelong. He did not hesitate to engage in criticism of public figures when he felt they were not being honest or when any other problems he perceived were made known.

Forest Grove continued to dwindle as Margaret sold off three additional pieces in 1870 and 1874, leaving only about eight hundred acres.[4] With Volney now head of his own household, John away at boarding school, and Preston Rose still a boy, Victor must have felt some degree of obligation to earn his keep, particularly as the eldest son in the family. Yet there is no record of how he spent his days following his final departure from the *Victoria Advocate* in 1873 or whether he was pursuing any income-producing endeavors other than contributing occasional pieces to the paper.

There are signs that he was becoming unreliable as his daughter's agent. When Julia Rose succumbed to yellow fever in 1867 along with her sister, Rosa, Victor's daughter had inherited the entire share of the Hardy daughters' Navarro property. As Julia Rosa Rose's legal guardian, Victor was responsible for appearing in court and filing an annual account.

Court records indicate that he failed to do so, and it was not until a citation was issued that he submitted the tardy report. His mother, likely realizing that she could not depend on her son in financial matters, petitioned the court to be released from any liability as one of his bond guarantors.[5] The court ordered Victor to file a new bond, which he failed to do.

Records indicate his behavior was pretty textbook for an addict. His drinking, womanizing, and violent streak were "scandalous" issues no one in the Rose family would openly acknowledge. These scandals, however, continued to grow as time went on. It is possible that such unsavory behavior could be contributed to the psychological wounds of wartime trauma.

Then in 1873, before she had turned seven, Julia Rosa inherited additional property when her grandmother died suddenly in Kansas. She became a woman of some considerable means in life.

In the spring of that year, Julia Rosa's grandmother Margaret Borland[6] decided to drive a herd of her cattle to Kansas to take advantage of higher prices. Along with her on the trail drive were her three surviving children and Julia Rosa. After reaching Wichita in June, however, Margaret became ill, fell into a "delirium," and died on July 5.

Her brother, James Heffernan, traveled to Kansas to settle his sister's affairs and make arrangements for the return of her body to Victoria, and presumably also brought the children home after he had purchased nine yards of silk for a shroud.[7] Her estate was subsequently divided equally among her three children. Her granddaughter, Julia Rosa, was taken in by an aunt and uncle named Jones.[8]

According to family accounts, Victor and his daughter spent time together at Forest Grove or when Victor was staying with Zilpa and George Overton Stoner, but the nature of their father-daughter relationship is unknown. As an adult, Julia would become active in both the Daughters of the Republic of Texas and the United Daughters of the Confederacy, possibly reflecting the influence of her father's interest in history. The only surviving description of Julia Rosa as a child comes from a niece who was named for her: "Cousin Julia took possession of me almost. I have been told that when I was a tiny baby, Cousin Julia would sit under the apple trees and rock me for hours. When Mother and Dad left the area, I understand that she cried for days. I didn't see her again, but when I was old enough to write I sent her long letters. She wrote long letters in return—they were almost like reading a story book."[9] Victor's daughter seems to have inherited her father's fluency in letter-writing. However, these letters have never been found.

On October 1, 1874, Victor married a second time, an event announced in the Galveston paper as the marriage of "Victor M. Rose, Esq., to Miss Ada Brooking."[10] Described by a niece as a tall, good-looking woman, Ada Adelaide Brooking was the seventeen-year-old daughter of Bivian Byron Brooking, an early settler in Goliad, and Johanna Miller Brooking, a Cherokee Indian whose father and brother owned a Wild West show.[11] Family accounts are largely silent about the actual circumstances of Victor's short-lived marriage, because the family strongly disapproved of the Brookings and also because the ensuing divorce and the reasons for it carried a stigma.

As in many families, embarrassments were "always hushed up . . . and they just never talked about those things."[12] The Brookings were outsiders at a time when the influx of new faces that came with Reconstruction provoked snobbery and distrust in the close-knit society of the old order. Furthermore, two of Ada's brothers were suspected of shady cattle dealings.[13] As a result, the whole family seems to have been regarded as "scamps" and "scoundrels" by the Roses.[14] [15] Yet in 1877, Victor's sister Margaret Malinda Rose would marry Ada's brother Robert Pitts Brooking. In Kathryn Stoner O'Connor's biographical sketch of her uncle, included in the 1961 reprint of Rose's *History of Victoria County*, there is no mention of Victor's second wife, Ada Brooking, a reflection perhaps of the family's enduring sensitivity about this episode in Victor's life.

Even with the family's blessing, the marriage would have surely been doomed, for the Brookings seemed to magnify Victor's dark side. They were referred to in Victor's book as "The Brookings Gang." Margaret McLean says, "I think the Brookings probably went out and did some things that were considered outside the law. If the family didn't want you to know something they just talked around it, and this was the case for me regarding the Brooking marriage."[16]

During part or all of the time that Victor and Ada lived together, they boarded with Ada's sister-in-law, Clara Nickelson Brooking, in Victoria.[17] In the spring of 1876, marital discord came to a head. According to court documents, Ada began to fear for her safety when Victor would fall into drunken rages and threaten her with bodily harm. In July, Ada fled to stay with her sister, Martha J. Brooking Wigginton, and then soon moved with her sister to Williamson County in November.[18]

On September 12, 1878, Ada filed for divorce, claiming that her husband was "guilty of excesses, cruel treatment, and outrages towards her of such a nature as to render their living together insupportable," that he was "constantly quarreling at, abusing and cursing" her, and that she was "compelled to keep someone with her to protect her from his threatened assaults as she was absolutely afraid to be alone with him."[19] She also charged that he had left her while she was sick without anyone to care for her. When he returned and she told him she could no longer tolerate this ill treatment, he replied, "God dammit—you can go to hell."[20] Ada's petition further stated that in mid-July 1876, Victor "committed the act of adultery with a colored woman by the name of Lou Ragland in Victoria County, Texas" and that he "took up with, lived in adultery and cohabited with" the woman.[21]

In a deposition, Clara Brooking stated, "I do not know anything about defendant's treatment of his wife, except that I only once heard him telling her 'to go to hell' and then he was intoxicated." She also said that on one occasion he had left his wife at midnight, taking his little girl with him. Ada's sister confirmed the pattern of physical violence and verbal abuse, adding that Victor "put up with a German woman who kept a saloon" during a time when his wife was "dangerously sick." In response to a question about the charge of adultery, she stated, "I only know this from the community talk. It was generally known and spoken of by everybody and certainly was true. He continued for several weeks to carry on this way." Clara's father, J. L. Nickelson, stated that the couple "were not very peaceable to one another. I know that defendant was sometimes drunk and also that he stayed away."[22]

The divorce was granted,[23] and at the time of the 1880 census, Ada was still living with her sister in Williamson County and using the name Ada Rose, even though she had petitioned for a return of her maiden name. Victor, now thirty-seven, was living with Zilpa and Overton Stoner and their children. He gave his marital status as divorced and his profession as lawyer.[24] Living at Forest Grove was no longer an option for Victor, as his mother had sold the last remaining acres of the property in September 1879 and moved to Llano County with her daughter and son-in-law, Zilla and Adam Summers, and her two youngest sons, John Washington Rose and Preston Robinson Rose.[25]

But Victor's hapless attachments continued. His sister later recalled two such incidents:

One day a woman came to our house. She said she was Victor's wife; he denied it. She called herself Mrs. Jackson. He would not have anything to do with her. She stayed there a while, and then left. She made the children call her Aunt Jennie. And then he was writing to a lady from South Carolina, I think. He decided he would go there and marry her and wanted O [Overton] to go with him, so at last O told him he would go. So they got ready, got packed, suddenly Victor would not go. So Overton was mad. . . . [A]bout one week after, Victor left, and said he married the woman. They came to our house, stayed a few days, then they went to Laredo to edit the paper for Mr. Penn. They didn't live together long. She went back. She seemed to be a nice lady. She wrote several times, then stopped.[26]

Whether "Mrs. Jackson" was connected with the Jackson family who took care of Victor in Vicksburg is unknown, nor has the South Carolina woman ever been identified. There were rumors that Victor had fathered a second child, but no evidence for this has been found. This incident may account for the rumor of an additional marriage.

So here we see the darker side of Victor Rose—the never-ending peccadilloes with women, unsuccessful marriages, alcoholism, adultery, and spousal abuse. However, he managed to either intermittently, or finally, pull himself together, and made a respectable living after the war. Zilpa Rose Stoner often kept her brother, because apparently he didn't stay married long or was gone for only short times and in between times he lived with her.[27]

By September 1879, Victor was no longer responsible for managing his daughter's property, having been removed as her guardian. This was no doubt the result of his alcoholism and mental upsets, as well as financial decisions that the family considered reckless and contrary to Julia Rosa's interests. Shortly after his marriage to Ada, he had petitioned the court for authority to sell his daughter's 962 acres in the Navarro tract. The court appointed Victor's brother-in-law, George Overton Stoner, as Julia Rosa's guardian.[28]

Around this same time, Victor became embroiled in a dispute that made his alcohol problem even more apparent to anyone who read the *Victoria Advocate*. The dispute arose over the terms of a transaction between Victor and a Victoria farmer named B. D. Culp. According to Victor, he had bought a sorrel mare and saddle from Culp, paid for it in full with no strings attached, and then several months later sold the mare and saddle to someone else. Culp claimed that the mare and saddle were part of a land trade and were on loan to Victor until the two could work out the specifics of the deal.[29]

The land, located in McMullen County, may have been part of his late wife's inheritance, as he had deeded the land to his daughter by this time. Culp—asserting that the mare and saddle were still his property and that, furthermore, he had made a payment on the land—made it known around town that he might charge Victor with "embezzlement."

The *Victoria Advocate*, in the issue of August 30, 1879, published a letter that Victor had written to the paper to refute Culp's "scandalous report" and "calumny." He included a sworn statement signed by his brother and mother saying that Victor had purchased the mare and saddle and that they were his property until he subsequently sold them. In the September 6 issue of the paper, Culp's own response was printed. He said that Victor had borrowed the mare and saddle, got drunk, and then sold them and that he had not seen Victor "unintoxicated" since that time. He added that he had not pursued embezzlement charges for several reasons: "This I did not attempt to do because of his condition when the act was committed, my past friendship for him, and the respect I had for his friends and relatives, but told them the facts to show them what he was capable of doing under the influence of liquor." Here we see Victor's reputation was indeed damaged at this time due to his drinking and bad behavior.

Victor struck back with another letter to the paper, accusing Culp of slander and stating: "I never proposed to give him the land in McMullen county for the mare. The statement is ridiculous and absurd. I considered the mare already paid for." As for Culp's comments about liquor being to blame, Victor states that Culp "is not my conscience keeper" and that therefore "I shall not notice his impudent remarks respecting my conduct, and no wise connected with the business in hand."[30]

In the midst of grappling with his demons—alcoholism, abusive behavior, adultery—Victor became increasingly preoccupied with his writing. By the late 1870s he was publishing poems in the Victoria paper under the pen name "Wild Rose." He possibly enjoyed cultivating the image of a dashing, romantic poet, as this nom de plume is attached only to poems and not the prose pieces that he published around the same time. If he hoped for some convenient anonymity in the wake of the Brooking debacle, it is unlikely that many readers were left guessing about the poet's real identity.

Meanwhile, Victor was also contemplating a more ambitious work: a history of his Civil War regiment. In August 1878 he had placed the following notice in an Austin newspaper: "Anyone knowing the whereabouts of the widow of Capt. Dunn, late of the Third Texas Cavalry, will aid a good cause by communicating the same to Victor M. Rose, Victoria, Texas."[31] Similar notices with the instruction "Texas papers please copy" were published that same month in the Galveston, Columbus, and Denison papers, and likely others in the region.

As Victor would later note in his prefatory remarks to *Ross' Texas Brigade*, Captain Rufus Dunn of Company F had drafted a history of the regiment at the request of General Ross. By locating his widow in Alabama, Victor was able to include information from the captain's surviving papers in his own work. Thus began a practice that Victor adopted when writing his historical works—gathering firsthand accounts, usually in the form of correspondence that would provide valuable source material. In his letters to potential informants, he courteously enclosed "stamps to pay postage on your reply."[32] We see his continued hard work to accurately preserve history.

Although this period marked a low ebb in Victor's personal life, 1878 was the year in which he saw the publication of his first book, a chapbook entitled *Los Despenadores—A Spanish Story*. The dedication to "General S.B. Maxey, U.S. Senator, soldier and a statesman," is dated October 15, 1877, indicating the probable date when the work was finished. According to an advertisement in the *Victoria Advocate* of July 13, 1878, copies were available at Marion Wheeler's drug store for twenty-five cents each.

A lengthy review in the *Austin State Gazette*, reprinted in the *Victoria Advocate*, provides good summary of the poem: "*Los Despenadores*, like Byron's *Don Juan*, is unquestionably original. While it scintillates throughout with flashes of poetic ratios, there is not a spark of Promethean fire visible. This of itself is saying much when so many poems 'smell of the lamp;' besides it is the distinguishing feature of the natural born poet."[33]

Although the poem has all the trappings of a conventional medieval romance in verse—with its remote setting, sentimentality, and the central figure of a knight—Victor gives the genre an unusual twist. Instead of a knight's heroic deeds, the narrative tells how the intrepid twelve-year-old Marie protects the middle-aged knight and vanquishes the secret society of the Despenadores,[34] one of the most bizarre aspects of the Spanish Inquisition. Thus the enemy is not a rival knight but an entire institution that has become corrupt. As Victor points out in his preface, the poem is not an indictment of the modern Catholic Church but of "crimes of a people" influenced by "ignorance and superstition that, fungus-like, sprung into existence throughout Europe during the long night of the 'Dark Ages.'"[35] Also unusual is Victor's interruption of the stately narrative to inject his own opinion about his preference for dark-eyed women with a devilish streak.

If this poem is an allegory about a weakened, defeated South, Victor implies that its hopes for recovery rest with the younger generation. The defeat of the South was often the subject of many of his writings.

All of Victor's careers involved writing in some form. In spite of his need to earn a living, particularly due to the death of Forest Grove, he was still determined to write and suffer the loss of a viable income from some other type of work. Apparently he lived with family for much of the time. He was also determined to continue to write poetry and record history at a time of great argumentation over how Texas history was to be written. He engaged in the revision of what he considered false Civil War history.[36]

Victor suffered dislocation and the loss of his career as a wealthy landholder, slaveholder, and casual writer. Like many Southerners, he had to make his own way under radically changed circumstances. He was also a victim of the psychological trauma of war. However, all cannot be blamed on Victor's wartime experience, as he manifested dysfunctional and violent behavior, along with many more positive talents and traits, early on in his life.[37] He was truly a Wild Rose.

Victor Marion Rose in his Confederate uniform, circa 1861. Courtesy of the Louise O'Connor Collection, Victoria, Texas.

Rose, not long after his return home from the war. Courtesy of the
Photograph Collection, Victoria Regional History Center, Victoria
College/UH-Victoria Library.

Victor Marion Rose sometimes used the pen name "Wild Rose." Courtesy of
the Louise O'Connor Collection, Victoria, Texas.

Rose married Julia Holmes Hardy in 1866. Courtesy of the
Louise O'Connor Collection, Victoria, Texas.

Julia Rose Anderson, daughter of Victor Marion Rose. Courtesy of the Ron Brown Collection, Victoria Regional History Center, Victoria College/ UH-Victoria Library.

CHAPTER FIVE

A Writer "Par Excellence"

1880–1889

THE DECADE beginning in 1880 was the most productive period of Victor Rose's career: he published seven books[1] in a ten-year span and, at the same time, edited newspapers in different regions of the state.[2] By 1880, he pulled no punches about his stance on current events and the people involved in those events. Here he really dedicates himself to leaving a truthful record of what he saw and was involved in during his time, in addition to useful commentary on other important historical events in his lifetime.

His work at this time was hard-core biography, history, poetry, and humorous works such as his *Kemper Kernals*. He claims some interest in writing about Mexico, but seems to have never gotten around to it.[3] He describes people's physical appearances, often in great detail. And, most significantly, in this era he begins to depict a reality that many were unable to accept. While he occasionally slips into sentimentality after the war, he starts to recover from the myth of the Lost Cause and pushes his reader forward into the new reality.

Kemper Kernals was a column written by Rose for and about Kemper City, Texas, in 1880. The former small community was located west off of the current Hwy 77 South before you reach the San Antonio River. Here are several excerpts from the column:

As your reporter receives some letters making inquiry respecting Kemper city, its location, population, business, etc., he embraces this medium through which to reply: Kemper is located, and in this particular enjoys a great advantage over its sister city, Anaqua, which follows the postoffice [*sic*] around. In this respect Anaqua is a lively town. The population of Kemper on the 2d day of July, A.D. 1880, approximated five hundred souls. As we cannot afford to enumerate the census of the city in conformity to the wishes of each question, we purpose [*sic*] giving the above figures as the population of Kemper until another census is taken. If the figures are too low fifty per cent will be added to the enumeration of the next census, which it is hoped will satisfy indulgent people.[4]

Mr. Peter Fagan has raised the biggest crop of alligator this year, and he's going to have fun gathering it—a regular jamboree of a time. Everybody and his wife are invited to attend and take a hand in the sport. Everything thrives on the bottom lands—cotton, corn, chills and cramp. The prairies produce grass and galls. The first is green, but I if you imagine the galls are green you had best not give expression to that fancy. The grass grows old, and dies in the winter. The galls never grow old, and Fagan's alligator never heard of one dying. This is a good range for galls, and a few more *manadas* would do well.[5]

The prevailing religion is the democratic, and Hancock's general order No. 40, is the shibboleth of faith. In Kemper strictly, there is no marrying nor giving in marriage. This is a custom adhered to since the solemnization of the nuptials of Col. San Antonio and Guadalupe.[6] The boss alligator attended that affair in company of a charming belle of the highly respected Mastodon family. A family that had great weight in public and private affairs of the day, but which, like the Stuarts, of Scotland, has become extinct. The "Boss," like Samuel J. Tilden, never married. Like Tilden, he never took his seat in the presidential chair. If there are other points of resemblance, our reporter will ascertain when he interviews the alligator, which will be after the matinee—provided the "Boss" don't hold his own. He'd interview him before the matinee, but previous engagements, etc.[7]

Making frequent appearances in the column is Old Simon, a fictitious African American that Rose employs as a vehicle for gentle social and political satire. Old Simon functions as the naïve observer whose comments unwittingly reveal the absurdities and shortcomings of society. Behind Old Simon's observations about the "perliteness" of politicians during the election season is Rose's distaste for political pandering, especially when it involved an attempt to win over black voters:

> Hit does do a man good dese days gist to got to Vic-tory an 'sociate wid de perlite foax. Candy-dates is de most perlitest foax outside ob de French dancin' master. Ef I wuz to lose my almanax, I could tell 'lection time wuz comin'. In de "off" times I's "Ole Simon;" spring 'lection, an I'm "Simon;" den arter awhile I'm "Simon Grubbs," and den Mr. Grubbs," and ef dey runs neck an neck on de home stretch, I'm good to be "Capt. Grubbs," I know ef hit wuzzent for 'lections and de wimmen foax, perliteness would pass away forever![8]

The character of Old Simon is often used to put forth Rose's personal opinions on a variety of matters. Here Rose uses dialect not only for humor but as a protection for his own, at times, unpopular ideas. His writing for *Kemper Kernals* shows his mischievous and humorous side to great effect.

In addition to his *Kemper Kernals* column, Rose also wrote letters to the editor of the *Advocate* on various topics. In April 1880 he wrote a long letter criticizing Homer S. Thrall's *History of Texas*, which appeared in 1876. It is interesting to recall that Rose had been Thrall's pupil at Rutersville College, although he refers to this association only obliquely, saying, "The untarnished reputation of Mr. Thrall for probity, honesty and truth, led all who enjoyed his acquaintance to believe that the 'history' would be all as represented."

What is significant about the piece is that it contains what may be Rose's earliest statement about his view of the historian's role: to be interesting *and* accurate. He faults Thrall for his terse, stiff style, saying that the author seems to consider anecdotes "beneath his province of historian; and that it is his especial privilege to be brief, unsatisfactory and *dull* to an intolerable degree." Rose then enumerates a number of errors in the book, including the account of the death of Travis at the Alamo: "He informs us that Travis fell early in the action; the siege continued eleven days, at the expiration of which . . . Travis ran a Mexican through with his sword." With tongue in cheek, Rose comments: "A lively corpse after eleven days sleep in death."

Rose concedes that most of Thrall's errors are inadvertent, but "the historian," he says, "should not only be absolutely true and correct in all his data, but he should be above suspicion."[9] In another 1880 letter to the *Advocate*, he again criticizes Thrall: "[N]o authentic history of Texas has yet been written; and . . . of all attempts, the latest—by Rev. H.S. Thrall—is the most signal failure."[10] Numerous times, especially in his newspaper writings, Rose would engage in polemics with numerous people on a variety of subjects.

Rose also shows his willingness to accept corrections of his own mistakes in print. In his letter of April 3 he had recounted an anecdote—which he attributed to a Victoria County judge named Truman Phelps—about the cannibalism of the Karankawa Indians and an incident involving Dr. Phelps, the judge's father. Judge Phelps immediately wrote to the *Advocate* a prickly letter to dispel any notion that his father had wandered into a Karankawa camp and been forced to eat human flesh: "My friend Mr. Rose has, no doubt, innocently mixed this story with what I told him of the unfortunate expedition of Perry in 1813–1814. . . . And he had done it in a manner that the reader would infer Dr. Phelps ate the foot, whereas neither he nor Foster did indulge in this dainty morsel. I write this to correct Mr. R's error, and hope he will be more careful if he should quote me hereafter."[11] In its May issue, the *Advocate* printed Rose's response:

> I accept the correction made by Judge Phelps in the last issue of the Advocate. . . . Of course the Judge's word is final and conclusive. His "correction" verifies my statement . . . to the *fact* of cannibalism, which fact alone, was the object sought to be demonstrated. The Judge converses in a very low tone, and my hearing not being very acute, I innocently confounded the details which he elucidated in his correction . . . I regarded Judge Phelps' testimony as conclusive of a long mooted question in regard to our early history, and, am pleased that the duty of correcting my inadvertent error led him to place his invaluable evidence on record. I assure the Judge, whom I have always looked up to as a venerable friend, that I would not wilfully misquote him, or any other person, under any considerations whatever.[12]

Again, his quick repartee and veiled observation that cannibalism was practiced shows the quick wit so characteristic of his writing style.

In consecutive weeks of December 1880 Rose published a three-part series in the *Advocate* titled "Incidents of the Past: Events Connected with the Army of Tennessee during the Late War." Although the articles appear under his byline, they consist mainly of the diary entries of his friend, Charles A. Leuschner,[13] with a few paragraphs of his own commentary. Leuschner, whose parents had immigrated to Victoria from Prussia, served in the 6th Texas Infantry and, like Rose, was a prisoner of war in Illinois.

At this time, Rose was gathering material for the history of his regiment and was aware of the importance of all firsthand accounts as historical documents. By publishing Leuschner's diary, Rose says he is intent on preserving a "succinct and continuous narrative" that will be "invaluable to the future historian of that period." At the end of the first installment in the series, Rose adds, "Victoria county should always feel pride in the deeds of this gallant company; as she sent no organization to the war who endured more hardships, and rendered more service than it."[14]

Rose's other submissions to the *Advocate* from this time reveal his views on a wide range of issues. In April 1880 he wrote a letter urging Victoria County planters to continue cultivating crops—cotton, sugar cane, wheat, and corn—and not jump on the bandwagon of stock raising, which was the trend following the war. In his belief that "agriculture is the basis of the social and commercial fabric," Rose echoed the agrarian ideal that was the driving force of the settlement of Victoria County as well as most of Texas. But he also recognized that traditional agriculture could coexist with the growing cattle industry: "The idea seems to have taken hold of many minds that the two industries of farming and stock-raising cannot be conducted in conjunction," he wrote. "This is erroneous, as in reality they should be inseparable."[15]

Rose's first book to appear in this period was *The Texas Vendetta; or, The Sutton-Taylor Feud*. Published in 1880, the book is ostensibly an account of the bloody conflict between two warring factions that carried out revenge killings in DeWitt, Gonzales, Karnes, and Bastrop counties. Significantly, it is the first attempt to chronicle the history of the feud and explain its causes. However, its real importance lies in its description of life in Texas under Reconstruction—a time of despair, rancor, and lawlessness. It is also a rare example for this period of a historical work that focuses on a specific topic in Texas history, as most nineteenth-century histories about Texas are general in scope.[16]

This historical study by Rose is valuable not only as an essay describing a famous Texas feud but, more importantly, as a description of life in Texas during Reconstruction after the Civil War. It was a very bad time for Southerners, as their way of life had been destroyed by defeat. In many cases, Northern officials grossly mistreated the former Confederates during this time of transition. Even where reasonable practices had been ordered by the Union administrators, they were too far away to check on their agents, sent as far away as Texas to conduct Reconstruction. There was much rancor and bitterness on both sides in the postwar years, and tempers flared. Over the South, Rose states, "hung the sword of Damocles."[17] He also refers to "the pernicious enforcement of the cruel 'Reconstruction Acts' of Congress."[18]

The primary source of the Sutton-Taylor feud was the irregular manner in which the nomadic stock raisers conducted their business. The free range was being fenced at this time. Before this, cattle had roamed free. We see that Rose used the word *dobies* instead of *dogies*, showing his ignorance of stock.

Lawbreaking became rampant, as outlaws and rustlers began to claim other people's stock that had wandered far away from their owners. This began to anger the landowners. Yet the outlaws and their activities were simply ignored by the Yankee authorities as more retribution was heaped on the South.

In this particular feud, the Taylors were headed by Pitkin Taylor, brother of Creed Taylor, a renowned Texas Ranger. Opposing them were the Suttons, headed by William E. Sutton, a former Confederate soldier, who had moved to DeWitt County along with his family. A rancher, Sutton also became a deputy sheriff in Clinton, Texas, and on March 25, 1868, shot and killed a Taylor kinsman named Charley Taylor when he tried to arrest him for horse theft. Later that year, on Christmas Eve, Sutton killed Buck Taylor and Dick Chisholm in a saloon in Clinton after an argument regarding the sale of some horses. When William Sutton became the recognized leader of the group, it made matters worse for the Taylor faction.

Rose describes this and other crimes as "high revel which the Confederacy gasped for breath."[19] The outlaws were becoming very wealthy under the administration. "No measure calculated to humiliate the pride of the rebel was lost sight of."[20] So the Taylors joined forces to resist this order, as they were to be killed on sight. Others, to protect themselves (as you were either pro- or anti-Taylor at the time) would neither feign allegiance to the Taylors nor do anything but ignore the entire issue. For years, killings related to this feud continued, leaving many no choice but to move to Mexico to survive. A compromise, at one point, was reached, but it soon broke down and hostilities continued.

Intent on giving readers an unbiased study of the feud, Rose includes official documents and eyewitness accounts representing both sides, along with reports from the *Victoria Advocate* and other papers, thereby preserving contemporary records of events. He even-handedly presents the cases of the much-hated figures who played a role in the feud.

The Sutton-Taylor feud finally came to the end with neither side being victorious. During these bloody years, the Taylor faction lost some twenty-two lives compared with thirteen fatalities among the Sutton faction.[21] Rose states that little remains to be said, and he attributes the cause of the unfortunate vendetta to two sources: the demoralization of the young men of that particular section as a consequence of the semi-nomadic life they led, and the unhinging tendencies of war: "Second—to the evil agencies set afoot by the military commanders, who saw in our own dissensions promise of radical concentration and power."[22] Once again, he provides readers with candid descriptions of a time of much societal disruption and frontier law.

As noted previously, Rose began gathering material for the history of his Confederate regiment in mid-1878, when he placed notices in state newspapers requesting help in locating Capt. Dunn's widow. By this means he was able to acquire Dunn's earlier draft of the regiment's history, prepared at the request of Gen. Ross, as the basis for his own work. Between 1878 and his completion of the manuscript, Rose also corresponded regularly with Gen. Ross himself and with other living members of the regiment to clarify points of fact. Whenever he wrote a historical piece, Rose attempted to gather information from as many people as possible who had firsthand knowledge of the events.

Ross' Texas Brigade; Being a Narrative of Events Connected with Its Service in the Late War Between the States was published in 1881. Rose, of course, dedicated the book to his subject, the distinguished Confederate general, and again chose a Latin phrase for an epigraph: *Conclamatum Est*—"It is all over." He is dead, past all hope.

As Rose explains in his prefatory remarks, he has based the history on not only the draft begun by Captain Dunn at the request of General Ross, but also on the memories of surviving members of the brigade, which, he says, "caused delay, and exacted much patience on the part of the author in arranging the many conflicting statements that had grown with time." He emphasizes his commitment to truth: "It is a solemn duty that the survivors owe to their fallen comrades to leave a truthful record of their deeds . . . for the truth of history must rest upon the statements of those who were contemporaneous with the events they detail."[23]

Rose's purpose in writing the book, in addition to recording the regiment's movements and engagements, is not to argue the Confederate cause: He says simply that the administration in Washington gave the South no alternative. When the North interpreted secession as a declaration of war and attacked Fort Sumter, enraged Southerners felt compelled to answer the call of duty and defend their honor. (The issue of slavery is not discussed.) Rose's purpose, rather, is to reveal the heroism of individual soldiers and officers, as well as volunteers, who faced overwhelming odds with uncommon bravery and altruism:[24]

> And right here, let the fact be recorded, that the best, the bravest, the hardiest, and less complaining soldiers were mere boys from sixteen to twenty years of age. . . . the Confederate forces did not exceed 9,000 men, and they mostly raw recruits, with no drill instruction, and but little discipline. The enemy probably numbered 12,000 men, but this disparity in numbers is of but little moment when the greater dispar-

ity of arms, discipline, and munitions of war, generally, are taken into account. The enemy was largely composed of United States regulars, and his volunteer regiments, too, were armed with the latest and most improved weapons.[25]

He also depicts the varied experiences of the soldier—the suffering caused by bad weather and scant food, the boredom during lulls in the action, the generosity of civilians along the route, the grinding fatigue, the harrowing ambushes resulting from a commander's tactical blunder, the solace of victory and the agony of defeat.

Although some passages may seem to glorify battle to the modern reader, Rose, in fact, uses dark terms to describe war, such as "[T]his human-created hell." The glory lies not in the battle itself but in the soldier's valor in transcending the hell that is war: "Ross and his braves were tried by ordeals that taxed to their utmost the highest qualities of our nature, and . . . they came forth from the fiery saturnalia of demoniac war as gold purified from the crucible."[26]

Ross' Texas Brigade remains an authoritative account of the 3rd Texas Cavalry's role in the Civil War, especially that of Company A. Victor's work captures a unique perspective—one that is closest in time to the events described—and modern historians still rely on the accounts in the book. E. M. Coulter, an eminent historian of the Confederacy, praises Rose's "frank and graphic" statements about the Confederate capture and pillaging of federal supplies in Holly Springs, Mississippi.[27] We see Victor's work lauded during his time and even today.[28] His work exemplifies two dominant characteristics of nineteenth-century Texas histories: a literary style and "memorial" intent.

The year 1882 saw a change of pace for Victor with the publication of a volume of poetry, *Demara, the Comanche Queen; and Other Rhymes.* In a May 14 issue of the *Galveston Daily News*, a reviewer called it a "beautiful little volume" whose contents "are numerous pieces on various subjects, patriotic and humorous, written in a sprightly manner, with excellent taste and patriotic spirit." The *San Marcos Free Press* of March 30, 1882, called it "a neat volume . . . containing quite a variety of readable verse" and went on to say, "Mr. Rose we have heard of for some years as a fertile and versatile writer of rare gifts." It should be noted that he was respected as a good writer even during his own time.

The book is dedicated to John Ireland of Seguin, a Confederate veteran, judge, and state senator who would later serve as governor from 1883 until 1887. In praising Ireland for his "masterly plea for a strict construction of our written organic law" and his "advocacy of the rights of the people as against favored classes,"[29] Rose is likely referring to Ireland's opposition, as a member of the 13th Texas Legislature, to the state's granting of money and land to railroad corporations in the 1870s.[30]

In the dedication Victor calls the poems "random verses," and his epigraphs for the book also employ the classic literary convention of author humility: *Dulce est desipere*[31] and *Vive la bagatelle*.[32] Despite the poet's self-effacing stance, the collection shows an impressive range of subjects, moods, and metrical forms.

Some of the poems were first published in the *Victoria Advocate* in 1879 and 1880, and possibly in years for which no issues have survived. The versions in *Demara* show minor changes in punctuation and diction that improve the poem, and occasionally Rose changed the title of the poem—for example, "M. Le Compt de Moranville" in the *Advocate* became "Victor Eude du Gaillon" in *Demara*. Three of the poems—"Ross' Men," "Battle of Oak Hills," and "The South"—had appeared in *Ross' Texas Brigade*.

Other poems in *Demara* are also set in the context of the Civil War. As in his history of the brigade, Rose uses these poems to praise the heroism of individual soldiers and not the Confederate cause. "Monody on the Death of General Robert E. Lee" is an ode emphasizing Lee's courage and leadership, despite the South's defeat.

The poem "Whitfield—Ector" honors two other Confederate generals, John Wilkins Whitfield and Mathew Duncan Ector, who reentered civilian life after the war and served as community leaders until their deaths in 1879. "General W.S. Hancock" is a tribute to the Union general who was the Democratic nominee for president in 1880. Rose commends him as a unifying force, a leader capable of healing the nation's war wounds: "The hero chief, by all the sections blest, Who knew no North, no South, no East, no West."[33]

Rose's tributes to military figures are not confined to officers, however. "In Memory of M.A. Windham" pays tribute to a first sergeant and close friend of Rose's in Company A who died in the Battle of Spring Hill. In *Ross' Texas Brigade* (where the name is spelled "Wyndham"), Rose calls him "one of nature's noblemen" and mourns him.

It would be difficult to say which of *Demara*'s poems might have been inspired by an actual love affair, but at least one, "Perdu,"[34] is possibly autobiographical if the note included at the end of the poem is factual and not a poetic device for effect. In the note Rose defends his decision to publish the poem on the grounds that, of the three persons described, he is the only one still living. Written in January 1864, which makes it one of the earliest poems in the book, "Perdu" concerns the poet's unconsummated love for a married woman and the pain of resisting "lawless love" in order to observe society's moral codes. Rose seems to have battled with this issue for much of his life.

Although the poet portrays himself as honorable, urging the woman to keep her marriage vows and praying that his friend, the husband, will not be subjected to the pain and disgrace of betrayal, Rose uses the explanatory note to condemn the social mores that prohibit and punish human frailties like sexual passion: "The perfect characters drawn in compliance with the demands of a prudish conventionality, have no place in human nature; and though we may write ourselves as saints ever so often, we may not in truth raise our natures much above the carnal desires of poor, fallen man."[35] Although this is speculation, the statement could be considered a peek into his inner soul and reference to some guilt about his own misconduct.

Another poem that explores morality, and especially its tension with forbidden love, is "Yussuf and Zuleekha," which is based on a Persian legend as well as the Old Testament story of Joseph and Potiphar's wife. Yussuf, enslaved by the king of Egypt, resists seduction attempts by the king's beautiful wife, Zuleeka, as "vile adultery." He persuades her to transform her erotic love into spiritual love. As is typical of Rose's imagination, the epic poem synthesizes Persian legend and Christian theology. It also reflects the Orientalism that was embraced by the nineteenth-century English poets, such as Byron's epic poem of 1813, "The Bride of Abydos: A Turkish Tale," which was originally titled "Zuleika." Although Byron tells a different version of the tale, it is written in couplets, as is Rose's poem.

The volume's title poem, "Demara, the Comanche Queen," is one of the best known of Rose's poetic works. This epic poem tells the story of a Comanche queen who rides a milk-white steed and whose realm stretches from east to west. She is "fair but ice-cold" and rejects all her suitors. A warrior named Pascal resolves to win her hand, to "woo with high chivalric quest the haughty queen." Within this framework of a medieval romance, the poet incorporates a real historical event, the Battle of Wichita Village, which took place in 1858 in Indian Territory when U.S. forces attacked a Comanche camp with the assistance of Wichita, Caddo, and Tonkawa scouts. Details of this battle also appear in *Ross' Texas Brigade*. In a prefatory note, Rose says while writing the poem, his thoughts often turned to a boyhood friend, George W. Pascal (Paschal), whose mother was a full-blooded Cherokee and who served in one of the few Union regiments from Texas.[36]

The story of the battle of Wichita is fascinating and contains firsthand accounts of L. S. "Sul" Ross, who was there. It also contains disturbing images of an assault on an Indian village, with painful descriptions of the fearful experiences of innocent women and children. One of the most fascinating stories is that of the rescue of a young white girl from the Comanche camp, who is rescued by Ross, later to become a wealthy man's wife in California. We are told the tale through of the eyes of Ross and Mohee, the Comanche, meeting in the midst of battle. The two were acquaintances from Ross's father's time on the frontier.[37]

Ross describes the Caddo, their allies, as brave, courageous, and faithful. The poem portrays Pascal as a Toncahna (Tonkawa) chief who, after being wounded in battle, has a vision in which Demara sings to him, yearning for her "errant knight." He is perhaps given a central role in the poem because of his mixed blood—for one theme of the poem is the threat posed to Native American culture by "the advance of the white man's course."

While in his newspaper columns Rose applauded industrial development and other signs of "progress" that were widely welcomed in the late nineteenth century, in "Demara" he reveals the dark side of "civilization"—or at least recognizes it as a double-edged sword. Just as the Deep South had been forced to surrender part of its culture in the name of moral advancement, so too was Native American culture unable to win the battle against ever-encroaching "civilization." It should be noted that in one particular interview, a Duwamish elder observed that there was no wilderness before the white man arrived.[38]

Rose turns to humor in poems such as "Ye Ancient Spinster's Prayer" and verses that mimic black dialect, as in "Dishy's Reply," "Reform of Marcus Aurelius Brewster," and "Old Simon's Version of the Fiery Furnace." Although this approach can seem patronizing to modern sensibilities, Rose captures the cadences of regional black speech just as he does in some of his prose anecdotes about Texans with heavy German accents.

In addition to a wide range of subjects, the poems of *Demara* show Rose's versatility in working with different metrical forms, such as the interlocking rhyme scheme of the madrigal, the unrhymed pentameter lines of blank verse, and the acrostic form of "Garfield," in which the first letter of each line spells out the subject's name. Yet Rose's overall preference is for quatrains and couplets. His real talent lies in his ability to draw upon and synthesize material from widely disparate sources, combining classical myths, medieval legends, biblical stories, and historical facts—a stylistic feature of not only his poetry but his prose.

The work for which Victor Rose is best known is his history of Victoria, first published in 1883 under the title *Some Historical Facts in Regard to the Settlement of Victoria, Texas: Its Progress and Present Status*. In 1961, long after the book was out of print, Victoria book collector and bookseller J. W. (Joe) Petty Jr. reprinted the book under a different but equally unwieldy title: *History of Victoria County: A Republishing of the Book Most Often Known as Victor Rose's History of Victoria*. In collaboration with Victor's niece, Kathryn Stoner O'Connor, who supplied a biographical sketch of the author, Petty had the book's original pages reset, line for line, with misprints corrected and endnotes provided.

Variant spellings of place-names were standardized, and an index of personal names was included.[39]

Rose dedicated the book to John (Juan) Joseph Linn, a member of Martin De Leon's original colony, a key statesman of the Texas Revolution, and Victoria's first mayor. Around the same time as he was writing his history of Victoria, Rose was helping Linn write his celebrated memoir, which was likewise published in 1883 as *Reminiscences of Fifty Years in Texas*. In a letter to the historian and journalist John Henry Brown, Rose wrote of Linn: "I was intimate with him from my earliest recollections to within a year or two of his death. I wrote his *Fifty Years In Texas*, and had in my possession for weeks all his papers."[40]

In his preface, written on February 28, 1883, in Kemper City, Rose states that the book "does not claim to be a history of Victoria County" —which explains his choice of title. Rather, he says, he is attempting to rescue "minutiae" from oblivion and, "without any claim to literary excellence," present these facts for "preservation, and perusal."

The first half of the book begins by tracing the origins of old Guadalupe Victoria—from the time of the seventeenth-century Spanish missionaries through colonization under Don Martin De Leon in the early eighteenth century and then through the period of revolution and annexation.

This is followed by a section on the Civil War era, in which Rose offers his condemnation of the conflict. Rose reveals his thoughts on many subjects, but by far the most startling were his views on slavery—which were very honest and unusual for his time and place.[41] He came to see slavery as an abomination and believed that slavery brought about the Old South's downfall. Southern slavery was based on economics and the deep-rooted belief that Africans were inferior human beings. Rose saw through this and rejected it, while others still held to these beliefs.

Rose also discusses Victoria's schools, churches, and civic organizations, often including inventory-like lists that reveal an urge to preserve even seemingly trivial scraps of the past, such as "List of Families Moved Away From Victoria"[42] and "Counted Cattle."[43] He reprints, for example, letters concerning the futile effort to dredge the Guadalupe River for navigation; muster rolls of Civil War units organized in Victoria County; lists of county post offices and voting precincts; and a directory of Victoria's bankers, lawyers, and physicians; hotels and restaurants; stables, saloons, mercantiles, and mills; and other business establishments—even the town's two undertakers.

Rose concludes the first half of the book with another reminder to readers that "this is not a history of Victoria, but merely an effort to save for the future historian data essential to such a work, and much of which in a few more years would have been irretrievably lost, as has, unfortunately, much already of great interest."[44] This statement is followed by his poem "Victoria Regina," composed in hexameters, the meter of Greek and Latin verse. He later included the poem, with a few minor changes, in *Celeste Valcœur*.

The second half of the book is devoted to biographical sketches of notable settlers and leading townspeople, with doctors, lawyers, merchants, ministers, and soldiers predominating. Mothers, wives, widows, and daughters are mentioned in the biographies of families or individual men, but only a handful of women—Bridget Eagan, Margaret Ingram, Annie Linn, Nellie Phelps, Fannie Halfin, Blundina Halfin, and Margaret Wright—are given separate entries, and only the last of these is discussed in detail. Margaret Wright appears to have piqued Rose's interest because of the hardships she faced and overcame. She was an "angel of mercy" during the Goliad massacre, lived in poverty at times, and apparently suffered life's vicissitudes in the process, going from "the executive mansion of Louisiana to the wilderness of Texas."[45]

These vivid profiles of Victoria's townspeople are some of the most engaging portions of the book for today's reader, consisting of a mix of useful genealogical information and entertaining anecdotes. With just a few well-crafted sentences, Rose can distill a person's character along with his or her lot in life. Many of his profiles even include dialogue, revealing his fondness for storytelling, as seen in his sketch of Richard Roman, a scout during the Mexican War.

The following favorable review of Rose's history appeared in the Galveston paper:

The matter contained in this work will doubtless prove of great interest to Texans generally. The volume, though rather diminutive in appearance, is certainly large enough to do justice to this particular county. Commencing as far back as 1600, the author chronicles all events worthy of notice, occasionally resulting in some thrilling and interesting narrative of the early days of Texas. Brief personal mention constitutes a good portion of the volume, written in a graphic and pleasing manner. The book is very neatly printed, and bound in black cloth, and no doubt will be appreciated by all natives of the State. The book can be had of A. Levi & Co., Victoria.[46]

At this point in time, Victor moved to Laredo, due to another scandal about a possible second wife. On July 28, 1884, the *Galveston Daily News* announced that "Mr. Victor Rose has to-day taken a situation on the editorial staff of the *Laredo Times* in Webb County." The *Laredo Times* was founded by James Saunders Penn, who began publishing the weekly on June 14, 1881. He added a daily edition in September 1883. A native of Clinton, Mississippi, he had moved with his family to Rutersville, Fayette County, in the mid-1850s. After serving in the Civil War, he operated a printing business in San Antonio before moving to Laredo, where he became one of the town's most vocal advocates for civic improvements.[47]

Apparently Rose and Penn became friends in Rutersville, perhaps as classmates. A few years after leaving the *Laredo Times*, Rose would write, "We would prove ungrateful to a cherished boyhood friend were we to stop here, for the Archimedian lever which has moved impossibilities at Laredo is the Times, James Saunders Penn, editor and proprietor, than whom a more honorable and conscientious man does not exist."[48] Before moving to Laredo, Rose would have surely visited Penn to arrange the printing of his *History of Victoria County*, which was printed by the *Laredo Times* print shop.

No issues of the Laredo paper have come to light from the period of Rose's tenure, but extracts from and comments about his *Laredo Times* editorials appeared in other state newspapers, giving some indication of the subject and providing insight into the style of Rose's articles from these years. He clearly wrote editorials in support of John Ireland, who was elected for a second term as governor on the Democratic ticket in 1884. The *Austin Weekly Statesman*, which opposed Ireland, commented on August 14, 1884: "The editor of the Laredo Times is turning humorist in his old days. He writeth now of the 'Jim crow papers that oppose John Ireland.'"

Rose had just arrived in Laredo to work at the *Times*, and he expresses optimism in his personal writings. He is surprised by the large size of Laredo and how it was a "regular Mexican town." He found it strangely appealing when he went down to look at the Rio Grande and "stumbled on some ten or twelve beauties in bathing. They flung their long hair to the breeze, shouted and capered about in the water like nymphs of old Neptune's dominion. They did not seem at all surprised at my mute admiration of their unveiled charms, but continued splashing water into one another's faces, laughing and shouting in Spanish. I went down and washed my face among them." The old rogue was at it again! His admiration for the ladies apparently moved with him.[49]

No doubt because of Rose's loyal and energetic political support, Governor Ireland rewarded him with an official position. The *Clarksville Standard* announced on March 11, 1887: "The Governor completed his staff today by appointing Victor M. Rose, of the Laredo Times, colonel and aid-de camp." Whether this position involved any stipend or specific duties is unknown—it may have been a largely ceremonial title. At any rate, from this point forward, Rose was often addressed by the honorific "Colonel."[50]

In his partisan editorials, Rose unleashed his fury against any political candidate, organization, or process that he considered corrupt. The November 6, 1884, issue of the *Galveston Daily News* noted that the *Laredo Times* had directed "a column and a half of invective" at a Webb County political organization, and the Galveston paper reprinted the following portion of the article: "The old leprous conglomeration of mephitic garbage and reeking corruption . . . has for a decade clung like an eating cancer to the body politic of Laredo. . . . The practices of this corrupt cabal, whose defiance of God is scarce less more pronounced than their utter disregard for mankind and decency, is a running sore upon the body politic of Texas, a disgrace to the civilization of the age, and it stinks in the nostrils of all good men. This spurious broth from the chaldron of the witches, whew! it stinketh!" Surely only Rose could have come up with this basket of epithets.

While writing for the *Laredo Times*, Rose showed interest in a wide range of subjects, not just political issues. His description of a Cinco de Mayo celebration in Nuevo Laredo was reprinted in the *Galveston Daily News* with the following remarks: "Brother Rose of the Laredo Times is a retired poet, but a sound of revelry by night causes his well-rested Pegasus to come tearing in from the prairie with ears and brush erect. He fraternized with the Aztecs across the Rio Grande, in what he calls the 'Cinco de Mayo in Nuevo Laredo; a gala day and a night of revelry, beauty, gallantry and patriotism.'"[51]

Because of his recognizable style—with its erudite vocabulary, exotic allusions, and byzantine syntax—Rose was often teased by other newspaper editors. In July 1886, for example, the *Galveston Daily News* speculated that Rose "didn't appear to be on duty" in the *Laredo Times* office. But soon after, it printed this response from the *Floresville Chronicle*:

> The News was mistaken, for Rose certainly perpetrated this: "To Field Marshal He-No Terrell, Duke of Fanfarande, Prince of Balderdash, etc., and so forth: Lonely son of the Mexican empire, the imperial eagle has sought rest at distant Miramar, and all the demi-gods and policies of that heroic era hath become pabulum of history, and here you are monkeying with Texas Supreme Court reports, and rounding up voters! To the Pantheon, me lud, the spirit of your imperial master beckons!!"
> Yes, that is Rose, sure enough.
> You may break, you may ruin the Times if you will,
> But the odor of Rose will hang to it still.[52]

For the most part, the gibes of other editors were good-natured, as they seemed to respect Rose's abilities if not always his views. During his second year on the job, the December 10, 1885, issue of the *Austin Weekly Statesman* proclaimed: "Laredo has the best daily paper of any town its size in the state, the *Laredo Times*." In 1891 the Corpus Christi paper paid this tribute to Rose long after he had left the *Times*: "It was Victor Rose, while editing the *Laredo Times*, who made the remark that there were only two things that would prevent a woman going to a dance, and they were death and no dance. Vic has been accused of being a good judge of human nature in his day."[53] Here we see Rose read and respected all over the journalistic world, even beyond Texas.

While still in Laredo and working for the *Times*, Rose published a biographical sketch of Walter P. Lane in the 1885 proceedings of the Texas Veteran Association. He had included a letter from Lane in *Ross' Texas Brigade* and perhaps he had even considered including a profile of Lane with the other biographical sketches in the book. His interest in Lane was rekindled when Lane became president of the Texas Veteran Association in 1884.

When Rose left Laredo in early July 1887, he had made a name for himself in the newspaper business. The announcement of his departure from the *Laredo Times* was reprinted in the *Galveston Daily*: "Mr. V.M. Rose, who has been connected with the Times for more than two years, left Friday morning for his old home at Victoria via San Antonio and Rosenberg Junction. . . . He is a forcible writer and doubtless will desire ere long to return to the tripod." The Galveston editor added, "The Times has lost the best Rose in its nosegay, but, as it intimates, he will not long shed his sweetness on the desert air. Victoria is called the city of roses, and Victor Rose is the biggest among them."[54]

It is unknown why Rose left Laredo, as his writings portray this as one of his happiest times. His humor was in full swing, and he appeared to enjoy the area and its culture. He had even made a name for himself. So why did he leave?

What we do know about Rose's time in Laredo from 1886 to 1887 was that he continued to lament the loss of the old-timers, did not enjoy social activities, and felt like a "stranger in a strange land." He believed that Mexico was inhabited by barbarians.[55] While enduring such struggles, he was also engaged in a continuing fight to publish his biography of Ben McCulloch.[56]

In a letter to John Henry Brown from Laredo, dated January 25, 1886, Rose states his intention "to portray Ben McCulloch as he was, and to excite emulation among our youth to practice his virtues; for I have often thought that no nobler exemplar could be chosen by the youth of Texas for all time to come, than Ben McCulloch, who to me seem different in many respects from all men. My father admired him fully as much as yourself, and the first contribution to the press from my pen was a defence [sic] of his conduct at the Battle of Oak Hill."[57]

Finally victorious in his pursuit of publication, in *The Life and Services of Gen. Ben McCulloch*, Rose writes, "McCulloch rallied his confused division and led them to the attack. He crushed Sigel at once, and then hastened with his regiments to the assistance of the closely pressed Missourians. Few men have ever acquitted themselves of a more delicate trust, imposing the very weightiest responsibilities, with greater credit to themselves than Gen. Ben McCulloch did on the field of Oak Hills, with which victory his name and his fame are indissolubly wedded. Studied misrepresentation has failed in its malign mission, and posterity will yet measure the fame of McCulloch in a mould of heroic proportions."[58]

In 1887, Rose made plans to take the proceeds from the Ben McCulloch book and buy the *Victoria Advocate*,[59] after some trouble getting the book onto shelves, as a Mr. Rust was not abiding by his promises to the point of theft of the book.[60] The book was published and distributed by August 1888.[61]

Rose remained good friends with *Laredo Times* editor James Saunders Penn. In 1889, when his own paper in Brazoria County was struggling, Rose nevertheless relished Penn's success: "The editor of the Old Cap notes with gratification the prosperity of the Laredo Times, on which press three years of his life were passed. There is not a more worthy man in Texas than Major J.S. Penn, the manager, nor a more promising city than the belle of the border."[62]

While editing the *Laredo Times*, Rose was also working on two volumes of poetry, both of which were published the year before he left Laredo. The first to be finished, judging from the date of its dedication, was *Celeste Valcœur: A Legend of Dixie*, which garnered this favorable review from the *Galveston Daily News*:

Probably this is the most interesting literary offspring of the Laredo lyric[ist] that has yet been cast upon the literary field. The story is laid in the South during the war, and is admirably carried out in form, wit and expression. It is something after the delicate rhythm of Owen Meredith's popular poem of Lucille, and in some portions partakes of the same beauties of composition, though it would be nothing less than hyperbole to place it on an equal footing or a favorable comparison. It is brimming over, however, with the mother-wit and vivacity of the author, at one time combining the free and easy mood in which Don Juan was composed by Byron, and then alternatively gliding into pathos and feeling. Though the author is wo[e]fully cramped for a proper word to make a rhyme at times, he generally comes out of the tussle with banners flying. On the whole the story is very prettily written and cleverly designed, and will repay one for a perusal. . . . It is nicely bound and printed.[63]

The reviewer's characterization of *Celeste Valcœur* as "most interesting" is something of an understatement, as the title poem is perhaps Rose's most original poetic work, a result of its fusion of different techniques and textures. Ostensibly the poem is about a woman's ill-fated choice between two suitors, set against the backdrop of the Civil War, but it also contains passages that run the gamut from sober reflections on the brutality of war to jokes about the creative process to rollicking parodies of courtship customs and social norms.

Celeste Valcœur is unlike much of Rose's other poetry in that it contains an abundance of colloquial words and phrases, yet Rose can deftly create sudden shifts in tone and mood, and all the passages dealing with Civil War battles are somber and moving. The war is personified as a raging giant, a "foul gnome," and a hell filled with Furies. The image of war as a monster is reflected in the book's epigraph, taken from lines in Virgil's *Aeneid* that describe the monster Fury: *Centum cinctus ahenis / Post tergum todis, fremit horridus ore cruento.*[64]

Celeste Valcœur has Rose's own original stamp—his characteristic mix of erudite learning, personal experience, and local history. As part of this style, he includes imaginary correspondence, such as his own letter to a friend, and excerpts from fictitious newspapers articles. Here we see an extremely varied range and deep knowledge of classical literature.

The other volume of poetry that Rose published in 1886 was the slim volume *While the Spell of Her Witchery Lingers, and Other Poems*. He dedicated the book to Abner Taylor of Chicago, a principal of the Capitol Syndicate and the chief contractor for the new Texas State Capitol in Austin. The dedication is uncharacteristic of Rose—Taylor was a Republican as well as a former Union soldier, and the project became embroiled in controversy before the building was finally completed in 1888. The sly tone suggests that this was perhaps a mock dedication—although it seemed to praise Taylor, Rose notes that Texans "will not fail to appreciate his work, which will require years to remunerate him." As part of the bargain, the state awarded the syndicate millions of acres of public lands—the kind of deal that Rose often opposed in his editorials.

The dedication of the title poem, on the other hand, is sincere. "While the Spell of Her Witchery Lingers" is a love poem to Melita Yglesias, a young woman whose mother was Helen Jessel, the daughter of Captain Laurent Jessel of Victoria and the granddaughter of Victoria's early surveyor, Jose Maria Jesus Carbajal, and the first owner of the land where Rose spent his boyhood. After the death of her first husband, a general named Yglesias who was executed by the Mexican army, she married Jean Marie Marius Perron, a native of Marseilles, France, who settled in Victoria in the late 1860s.[65] Victor must have been courting Melita around the time he composed the poem, dated 1886, for Victor's niece says that she found the following note on the flyleaf of an old book: "V.M. Rose in 1886 proposed marriage to my sister, Melita Perron. He was rejected."[66] In addition to other love poems, *While the Spell of Her Witchery Lingers* contains short lyrics on a variety of subjects that were likely written over a long time span.

One of the most original poems in the collection is "The Chapparral Cock." The poem begins as an ode, with the poet addressing the roadrunner in mock-heroic terms. "O, clipper built on legs of speed, Thou feather'd frigate of a desert steed!" Then he envisions the bird as something "the size of nursery bugaboo" that could devour politicians who advocated the caucus system[67] that Rose despised.[68]

The final poem in the volume—and perhaps the earliest—is "September, 1867," written about Julia's death. Although the date of her death is unknown, the title of the poem seems significant. Victor signed the poem with a date of September 9, so he may have written these lines hours or days after she died. Not published until 1886, it conveys his deep grief over losing his "sainted young wife," his "darling departed." After leaving the *Laredo Times*, Rose occasionally wrote for the *Jackson County Progress*, published in Edna by Victoria native, Frank Dickson.

Undoubtedly, Rose's most well-researched and painstaking work during this time period was his aforementioned biography of Ben McCulloch. It cannot be pinpointed when Rose first conceived the idea of his biography on McCulloch, but McCulloch was a figure who loomed large in the Rose family. When Victor was a cadet at the Texas Military Institute in Rutersville, Ben McCulloch presented the school superintendent with "an elegant Turkish scimeter" and made a lasting impression on the youth.[69] Rose once noted that Judge Rose "was always a great friend of Gen. McCulloch, and wrote me soon after the battle of Oak Hills to make myself known to him; but my modesty prevented me from doing so."[70] In 1883, while Rose was still in Kemper City, he had boldly written to the former president of the Confederacy about the McCulloch project. Jefferson Davis replied, "Ill health and many pressing engagements will not permit me to answer as fully as I would wish to the questions you proposed," but he added, "I am glad that you are about to engage in a biographical work to do full justice to McCulloch."[71] For the next five years, Rose would doggedly gather material about his hero from as many sources as possible.

Throughout the project, Rose sought information and advice from newspaperman and historian, John Henry Brown, who became his mentor. Brown, more than twenty years Rose's senior, had lived in Victoria in the 1840s and worked for the *Victoria Advocate*. He later edited newspapers in Indianola and Galveston and then settled in Dallas in the 1870s. In the 1880s he was working on various histories that have become Texana standards. Most significant for Rose's purposes, Brown had been Ben McCulloch's aide-de-camp until the general's death in 1862. Brown was then transferred to the staff of Ben's younger brother,

General Henry Eustace McCulloch, who returned to his home in Seguin after the war.

To write a solid biography of McCulloch, Rose had to account for several periods of the general's life, of which he had scant knowledge, including McCulloch's boyhood in Tennessee, his service at San Jacinto during the Texas Revolution, and his career as a Texas Ranger fighting hostile Indians and protecting the new Republic of Texas from guerillas in northern Mexico.[72]

As Ben McCulloch's brother was still living, Rose was able to obtain rich details about Ben's family and early life from him—a Mr. Henry McCulloch in Seguin. Henry would have preferred to see John Henry Brown write the biography of his brother, as he confided to Brown in late 1883: "I know in advance that his life writ[t]en by you would be much more satisfactory to me and the public, if for no other reason, there would be heart in it, from a recollection of the many scares through which you had passed together in defense of a common cause and which had drawn you together more like brothers than friends, but as circumstances had prevented this I could only accept the next best prospect to get it done, and as our friend I know that Rose will do his best."[73]

But Brown paved the way for Rose, commending his friend to McCulloch by saying that "Rose is a good writer" and he had no doubt that the book would give a "correct history of the war operation in Ark. and Ms."[74]

Rose ends the biography with a long chapter on John Henry Brown. This was not simply a courtesy to Brown, who had provided so much help with the project, but a structural device to provide continuity and context for the main narrative, which would have otherwise ended abruptly and darkly. Since Brown's life paralleled much of McCulloch's, this chapter has the effect of extending the narrative in time, describing events leading up to the war and after.

In the summer of 1887, while he was waiting for the McCulloch biography to appear, Rose was in Edna, in Jackson County, working on a description of Jackson and Wharton counties for a special edition of the *Jackson County Progress*. After completing that project, he told Brown that he would "cast about for some journalistic position."[75]

The *Galveston Daily News* picked up many of Rose's stories from around the state, thus showing his widespread appeal and the reach of his writings. In these pieces, he expresses his disappointment in politics and some of the candidates of the times. The Republicans gained increasing power, and Rose feared a return to Reconstruction: "[T]he new party [Republican] will inject into the central monster [national government] the spirit of paternalism, which originally germinated in the hot beds of European communism. Thus we are drifting further and further from the ancient landmarks, and the time is not far distant when the republic of Jefferson will be regarded as creature of the fancy, as visionary as the Utopia of Sir Thomas More."[76]

During this period, Rose's "Jake's Quadrille" is regrettably a slide back into the "watermelon eating and google-eyed" descriptions of blacks. He went on to rise above this take later in his editorials and writings for *The Old Capitol*, progressing as a thinker and writer beyond the ways of the Old South.

In his prose writings, we see editorials and articles that he wrote while serving as editor of the *Victoria Advocate*, *Laredo Times*, *The Old Capitol*, and the *Galveston Daily News* at various times in his career. Nineteenth-century spellings were retained, but Rose's idiosyncratic spellings were clarified wherever confusion might result.

Here we see Victor in his greatest years of writing, producing a wide array of works in various styles. During these times, he covered diverse subjects, changing his philosophies from time to time, but only showing a leaning toward liberalism occasionally. He impressed Texas and other parts of the country as a capable and interesting writer (see appendices 3 and 4 for a selection of his writing). The need to earn a living had apparently helped pull him out of a bad patch after the war, and in that space, he went on to produce a wide array of thought-provoking and distinctive pieces of writing.

CHAPTER SIX

The Old Capitol
1887–1889

AT SOME point in 1887 Rose was in Edna, Jackson County, on a trip related to the newspaper, *The Edna Progress*. Around this time he owned or edited several publications, in addition to doing some ghost-writing.[1]

Rose then moved to Columbia, Texas,[2] to publish and edit *The Old Capitol*, a newspaper that made advancements in the content of small local newspapers. His extensive involvement with Mordello Munson, a businessman and son of a well-known early settler who arrived with S. F. Austin in 1828,[3] resulted in the founding of the newspaper, which is chronicled in the Rose-Munson letters (1887–1890). *The Old Capitol* was underwritten by Munson with Rose as the editor. Its purpose was to promote Munson's home county, Brazoria, and specifically to fight for the establishment of a deepwater port at Brazos in opposition to Houston and Galveston.[4]

Rose named this newspaper *The Old Capitol* because Columbia was once capital of Texas. The only remaining copies of *The Old Capitol* are for the years 1887 to 1889. However, these give a good view of what Rose was like in his second career as a newspaper man. A large part of each paper promotes the deepwater port for Brazoria. The remaining pages are filled with news and educational material of all kinds.

A few months after his McCulloch biography was published, Rose faced a milestone in his personal life. His twenty-one-year-old daughter, Julia Rosa, was married in September 1888. The *Jackson County Prog-*

ress announced in its September 5 issue that Wallace Anderson had wed "the only child of the celebrated poet and historian of Texas, V.M. Rose."[5] Wallace Anderson was an eighteen-year-old farmer from Thomaston,[6] a railroad shipping point in eastern DeWitt County near the Victoria County line. Thomaston's proximity to Victoria allowed Julia to make frequent visits to her hometown by train, which were reported in area papers.[7] Here Rose is once more described as a celebrated writer.

He appears from his work in the newspaper to have recovered from the necessity to laud and suffer the fate of the Confederacy and the Old South. There is no further mention of the subject or writings about it, with the exception of a few pieces on Ben and Henry McCulloch. As noted, he forever praised the brave generals of the South.[8]

Rose was still quite young, not even fifty years old, but apparently his health was not good, mainly due to his war experiences and wounds, as well as his bout with yellow fever. Regardless, he had once again moved and started a fresh career.

While he was with *The Old Capitol*, he was constantly performing research. Letters from this time period reveal Rose's preoccupation with gaining patronage and funding in order to publish and distribute his books. They also indicated the precarious financial conditions he was struggling against. At one point, he proposed that he would be able to share the costs of starting the newspaper by using the proceeds of the sales of the biography of Gen. Ben McCulloch.

The newspaper was the most influential type of literature in the Old South, as news was the least thing these newspapers considered worthy of note—content was often promotional or editorial.[9] However, Rose broke from the typical pattern of the day, discussing far-reaching subjects in his newspaper columns. We see this trend consistently throughout his articles.[10]

The Old Capitol has the best collection of Rose's postwar works and shows his change in thought and writing quite well on a number of subjects.

His articles in *The Old Capitol* cover many subjects and were amazingly thorough—far more sophisticated than average small-town newspapers of this era. There was always local news of the social and business variety, but the bulk of each edition was widespread in its content. He taught history in each edition in some way and corrected historical inaccuracies, always one of his main interests throughout his writing life. He also began to add women's news and writings, another new innovation for the late 1800s in small town Texas.

Although *The Old Capitol* was a promotional publication, the real business of the newspaper was to print editorials. Rose always had something to say. He often corrected the myths about the South and the war, and spoke to the issues of the times culturally, historically, and socially. His newspapers were more inclusive than most. Widely scattered articles on many subjects—articles praising heroes of the past, apologies for delay of delivery of *The Old Capitol*, death notices and snippets of mild social gossip, numerous advertisements, historical teachings and information—filled the pages of *The Old Capitol*.

From the letters to the editor in Rose's newspapers and his correspondence with prominent people, it is apparent that many followed his writings and opinions all over the state—and occasionally out of state. His columns and writings often appeared in the *Galveston Daily News* and had appeared in some Northern newspapers also.

His eloquence and wit are ever present in his writing: "Unfortunately, the good people of Brazoria are not only divided but bitter in sentiment to their opponents. My observations there led me to believe that it only required some act of imprudence on either side to cause bloodshed."[11] Another humorous quote appears in *The Old Capitol* December 7, 1887, edition:

> Advertising maketh the heart of the publisher glad, being as they are, the life of concern.
> Don't feel any delicacy in shoving your "ads" boldly to the front in large display type.

> Victor Rose, Editor.

A number of ads from Victoria were coming to *The Old Capitol*, and he often made contact with his hometown for much of his life. He also remained in touch with even more distant places, reporting news from around the globe. The out-of-state news he reported often came from other newspapers that he subscribed to, but it would be interesting to know how he got news about Turkey and other distant places.[12] It is known that Professor L. M. Disney apparently had an extensive library that he made available to Rose.[13] We can only assume this was a main source of his broad-reaching articles, as encyclopedic sources for research were not readily available in those days.

Rose's reports were as worldly as they were humorous. The way he reports on even sad events is, in a way, full of his characteristic wit. For instance, one particular edition of *The Old Capitol* contains an article stating that a judge committed suicide from "aberration of mind and dissipation."[14] Rose had an unusually comedic take on things, and often found news of an unusual nature to report.[15]

At one point, *The Old Capitol* humorously heralds its own "[g]ood looks and spicy contents," claiming itself to be "the paper [that is] almost as handsome as the editor." Rose replied: "That takes the bakery, Sloan, the handsome editor part. An' you love me, Hal, no more of that."[16]

In addition to humorous pundits such as these, *The Old Capitol* often contained "how-to" instructions on many subjects. Rose frequently notes the activities of Victoria people, such as a notice that one J. A. McFadden was asking for drop-in railroad rates to haul cattle. It is hard to determine if this was because Victoria was a center of interest and activity at the time, or if Rose was just staying in touch with his home. It is interesting to note that there could be, at times, heavy influence brought about by wealthy and influential people, and Rose did not back away from making this known. It was always done in a subtle way without preaching about it. With his mention of McFadden asking for lower rates, here Rose implies that some kind of pressure might be applied to secure a rate drop. This would not have been unusual for the times.[17]

The February 24, 1888, edition of *The Old Capitol* is full of humorous items. Rose refers to the name of a Houston newspaper as the *Evening Slopbucket*, and describes the name as euphonious. "Looming and Blooming" was the title of an article on the Brazoria harbor project. Then he slipped over to the city of Austin, referring to the Aransas Pass Railroad as a pet of Stephen F. Austin. "Seems that it would be better to pet one from Austin to the Brazos."[18] Here we see more reasons why Rose dislikes Austin.

Proceeding to Attorney General James Hogg, he states that Hogg is engaged in throwing a legal bomb into the Texas Traffic Association. "He seems inspired by faith in the ox cart as against railroads. Excess of legal bombshells is worse than no law."[19] Here there are heavy implications that Victoria and Aransas Pass are vying for the railroad against Brazoria. Yet further research reveals no correspondence in Rose's papers between his Victoria friends and relatives on this subject.

Rose used the word "dunderheads" when he was talking about poor thinkers, a word often used by later generations of his family. The *Victoria Advocate* was referred to as "The Old Battle Ax." The list goes on, with Rose at one point lambasting a lecture by O. M. Roberts that stated that all problems were due to "n———s."[20] By this time, Rose had completely recovered from this attitude about freemen, as he shows quite often in his newspaper articles.[21]

He often reports on news in Ireland and on the Irish. Humor abounds throughout all editions, and he, by this time, had truly put aside the "Lost Cause" issue. At this stage in his career, he writes sharply at all times, having put away the ponderosities of the old Southern writing style. He was almost always full of humor and looking for the absurd and ridiculous side of life and humans.

Often quoting Mark Twain in his newspaper, he constantly questioned the laxness and lack of enlightened thought from government, as well as many others.[22] Strangely, considering his stance on Stephen F. Austin, he printed a two-part article on Austin when he returned from Mexico in 1836. There is no comment from Rose on this subject. However, he does expound the virtues of dewberries and cream.[23]

On April 21, 1888, he includes a column on the eccentric wife of a well-known professor in the "Women's News" section. A week later, by April 28, he is seriously on about several subjects: He notes that the adherence between Henry McCulloch and Treasurer Lubbock waxes hot.

He states that Laredo has a spicy newspaper. (Since Rose was a bit spicy himself, it would be fun to know what that was all about.) His writing becomes highly animated and at times sensational; he pulls no punches.

Rose often describes other cultures with an eye to educating. One edition of *The Old Capitol* includes a history of how Mexicans got to China. This type of information surely came from his access to Professor Disney's library.[24]

The front page of the June 16, 1888, issue of *The Old Capitol* depicts nothing but advertising for Brazoria, the deepwater port, and the advantages of living in that county. On June 23, he finishes the month with lots of articles about other cultures and countries. His range of interest is ever expanding and filled with intrigue.

With heavy rains in June, Rose went on to say in the July 7 edition that politicians took too little notice of or interest in farming. Again, as a journalist he commits to bringing problems to the attention of the reader on both the community and worldwide level.

Throughout June, we see much about the deepwater port for Brazoria being almost assured by the election of W. H. Crain[25] in Victoria. From this edition on, all of the newspapers contain rallying cries and laudatory remarks for Crain. W. H. Crain was held in high regard by Rose due to his support of the Brazos project.

Clearly, Rose does not shrink from putting his opinions out there and receiving criticism from others in his newspaper. One particular issue goes on to present a letter from Patricio De Leon, a grandson of Martin De Leon, congratulating those who supported the Brazos Harbor project. De Leon continues by lauding W. H. Crain as the "Cicero of the Southwest."[26] Jokes and funny stories are seen throughout *The Old Capitol*.

In the July 28 issue, Rose notes that Barney Gibbs and his gang are monkeying at the same old stand in 1888 that James Power was using at Aransas Pass City in 1837.[27] It is hard to determine exactly what this means, but it was definitely derogatory to Gibbs. In Hobart Huson's *History of Refugio County*, the only mention of Barney Gibbs, former attorney general and lieutenant governor, is about him buying a mansion from Hall and converting it to a hotel.[28] The "monkeying around" must have referred to the attempts by Power, Joseph Smith, Henry Smith, and others to build coastal towns, with some failing and some lasting for a time. This had been a time of much land speculation and attempts at building towns and coastal ports, much corruption, and less than fully lawful attempts at winning the game.

By August 3, 1889, he notes *The Old Capitol* is ready to fire him and now takes note that W. H. Crain, formerly a big supporter, had done nothing to help him with this issue.[29]

The newspaper of September 1, 1888, tells of Crain's support of the canal to Galveston from Brazos. Crain contacted the president and the bill was approved. Later, we see Rose insisting that Crain was involved in getting him out of the newspaper.[30] This mystery was apparently never solved.

Once again in this issue, Rose related to some form of madness, as was his wont. He loved crazy stories and had a great interest in bizarre humor. This article tells of a statue in San Antonio that was defaced by a Masonic symbol. It was a statue of the Catholic saint Teresa. General C (name not given in article) destroyed the statue as sacrilegious. It was stated by Rose that it must be the oldest Masonic symbol in Texas. Then Charles Yoakum[31] comes back refuting the claim by Rose as to the antiquity of the Masonic symbol. He then counsels Rose to read the treatise of Leo Taxil on the history of Freemasonry. This whole thing proved to be a hoax.[32]

Later that month, a reverend in the African Methodist Church is described as a "very intelligent Negro." More than once we see Rose include an article about some African American who has made advancements after Emancipation.[33] We continue to see Rose make advancements in his thoughts and opinions about the freed blacks. More and more he notes the achievements of the freed slaves and other freemen. There is a feeling in his writings that he also takes pride in their advancement.

Rose continued to actively report controversial situations and people in his later career. The Hon. W. H. Crain was a congressman in the district and highly regarded in the Victoria area. He apparently greatly upset someone named J. V. Spohn of Encinal while speaking out against a protective tariff while in Laredo. In *The Old Capitol*, October 27, 1888, Rose writes:

> At the recent republican rally in Laredo in support of Col. Brewster for congress, Mr. J.V. Spohn; of Encinal, alluded to Hon. W.H. Crain as a "traitor to his district," as a "dishonest recreant, etc.," all of which was wholly gratuitous and without particle of foundation. In every speech made by Crain in Laredo he came squarely out against a protective tariff. He has proved recreant to nothing. Spohn's ilk have always opposed him, and it would be interesting to know by what species of ensuistry they ever laid claim to Crain's fealty; for there must have existed fealty where recreancy is charged. The Spohn ilk are "Showalterites" in a virtuous indignation cast. If they could command returning officers, and foozle county judges to go behind the returns, and install the defeated candidate, as they did once, there might be something in this much ado about nothing. But all that political rottenness is past, and can never again be repeated, even in Hidalgos county, perhaps. William Henry will very easily brush out of his path any obstacles placed there by the Spohn ilk; for his majority will be greater than ever before.

Often we see Rose's ability to take as well as give. He publishes or prints all attacks on his stances without fail. From the *Richmond Democrat*, October 6, 1888: "The Columbus Old Capitol publishes a poem entitled 'Battle of Richmond.' The fact that the author is a 'fair lady' prevents us from saying what ought to be done with one who inflicts such dreary, weary, miserable rhyme upon the unsuspecting public. *Oh, mores, O, temporal*."

On November 17, there is an article noting that the *Victoria Advocate* seems to be training a young colored statesman whom it declares to be a heap smarter than Cuney.[34] This notice and several others on successful blacks again show his positive attitude about blacks in general —he is favorable and accepting of them as intelligent human beings.

During his time with *The Old Capitol*, Rose was apparently acting as a real estate agent and confidential agent, as well as editor and business manager of the paper, although he had apparently never met Munson.[35] He writes Munson that he may break with the syndicate, advocating for Brazos River improvements for "the greater good of the people," and to keep *The Old Capitol* afloat. He then declares he will have to break his commitment to the paper, which was started largely to support this project and move it to Dallas.

In August 1889, Rose relates to the hopelessness of continuing to publish *The Old Capitol*. The press and type would have to be sold to pay the stockholders. He goes on to tell Munson that he considered this the best plan and acknowledged a debt of gratitude to him.

The Old Capitol was for sale, and at this time Rose claims to have been falsely accused of blackmail. Surely this was not another of his peccadilloes. We have no way of knowing what brought this commentary on or what the end result of it was. However, this was in the time frame of his loss of the paper, reportedly because of financial troubles.[36] His writing and editing at this time were some of his best output, and apparently this was a time where his scandals had ceased and his range had expanded greatly.

CHAPTER SEVEN

The Final Years

1890–1893

WHEN Rose resigned from *The Old Capitol* in August 1889, he stayed on for a while in Brazoria County, probably because he had no immediate prospects and was busy finishing his next work, a poem about Stephen F. Austin. In a September 1889 letter to Henry McCulloch, he wrote, "I am now rusticating for a brief spell on the plantation of W.T. [*sic*] Terry whom you knew in Victoria County; but hope soon to be in the journalistic business; but not in Sissyumbia, which is being Yankinised at a fearful velocity."[1] Terry was apparently an old friend who had moved from Victoria County to a plantation at Sandy Point in Brazoria County in the 1880s.[2]

In the same letter to McCulloch, Rose says that he intends to publish a "biographical sketch" of him that autumn and asks for clarification about McCulloch's role in an 1863 incident involving the Jernigan Thicket, a haven in northeastern Texas for Confederate deserters and outlaws. It is likely that Rose envisioned a companion volume to his earlier biography of Henry's brother. The unpublished manuscript of the Henry McCulloch biography existed as recently as the 1970s in the files of Kathryn Stoner O'Connor, Rose's niece, but it subsequently disappeared and is believed to have been stolen or thrown away.[3] The year in which it was completed is not known, but it was Rose's last historical project. A surviving short piece by Rose on Henry McCulloch appears in appendix 2.

Rose's very anti–Stephen F. Austin stance and subsequent small book attacking Austin[4] was the result of much correspondence with John Henry Brown in reference to Guy Bryan and his pro-Austin stance. The correspondence between the two began in February 1889, and continued through December of the same year. Bryan is the nephew of Stephen F. Austin.

Rose begins with a letter to Brown, laying out his annoyance with Bryan, who said that Austin was the author of the Mexican Constitution of 1824 and an advocate of independence. Apparently, Bryan had announced that he would write a biography of Austin when he got out of the legislature.

In attacking Austin, Rose notes he had tried to save Bryan from putting out a false history, but instead made an enemy of him. Rose refers to him as "floundering in the bog of ignorance to his doom."[5] He says the "smothered truth will be aired."

In the Balances was published in 1890 as a small book. This political poem is dedicated to Henry Smith, the first American governor of Texas and leader of the Independence Party. This party, in 1835–36, opposed the Mexican policy of Stephen F. Austin. The book contains many sly asides, such as the mention on page 9 of Guy Bryan as an "enemy" of the Smith defenders, and a positive reference to Rose's friend, historian John Henry Brown. The book also mentions many famous figures of that era, such as Napoleon and Victor Hugo, who Rose considered a serious antihero.[6]

Some, such as G. W. Fulton, thought Rose's attack on Austin to be impudent.[7] Thus the jury was still out on whether Rose was right about Austin. However, Gregg Cantrell does leave an ambiguous comment indicating that others besides Rose were of this opinion and that Rose's hatred of Austin appeared to know no bounds, especially given the veracity of Rose's attack on Stephen F. Austin in *In the Balances*.[8] Cantrell referred to this work as "splenic."

The source of Rose's animosity toward Austin is not so difficult to understand. The promotional campaign of Guy Bryan rankled Rose as a historian. More significantly, Austin the empresario may have been a proxy for the Bryan kin, who, Rose felt, had forced him out as editor of *The Old Capitol*. It should be remembered that *The Old Capitol* was the result of Rose's own initiatives, and it was the first newspaper that he had edited solely on his own. The loss of *The Old Capitol* would have been a heavy blow to his pride, his dignity, and his reputation. Furthermore, Rose's "spleen" toward Austin was not an aberration: his newspaper editorials often excoriated politicians and what he saw as their wayward viewpoints and behaviors.

Along with their flashes of eloquence and wit, his editorials could be strident. Schooled in the works of the classical orators, Rose knew how to wield invective for rhetorical effect. Behind his attacks in print, one can sense the same combative impulses that had led to acts of physical aggression when he was a younger man. As he aged, he began to use his fists on paper.

If Rose finished a biography of Stephen F. Austin, it has been lost, but it was surely what lay behind these words in the dedication of *Stephen F. Austin in the Balances*: "Truth demands restitution, and this is the initial step in securing that desideratum, but not the *last*."[9] In fact, in his subsequent newspaper writings at Emory and Myrtle Springs, Rose never let go of Stephen F. Austin as a topic worthy of criticism.

By May 1890 Rose was in Emory, the seat of Rains County in northeast Texas. In a letter to John Henry Brown on May 10, he wrote, "I will commence the publication of a paper at this place within the coming fortnight."[10] And in its issue of June 17, 1890, the *Fort Worth Daily Gazette* carried this announcement: "Victor M. Rose, an editor of twenty years' experience, is preparing to issue a newspaper at Emory, Rains County, which is to be called the Emory Star." More than a decade earlier, regional newspapers had announced that a new Democratic paper called the *Star* would begin publication in Emory, with a "Capt. H.E. Monroe, formerly of the Greenville *Herald*" as its editor.[11] As there is no evidence that this earlier Emory paper ever got off the ground, it would not be surprising if Rose gave his paper the same title as a nod to history.

No issues of the short-lived *Star* have survived, and only a few extracts taken from Rose's articles can be found in other papers. In the fall of 1890, after roughly six months of editing the *Star*, Rose precipitous-

ly decided to move the newspaper to another location. In its issue of
November 24, 1890, the *Fort Worth Daily Gazette* announced: "We regret to learn that Victor M. Rose contemplates moving the plant of the
Emory Star to some other town. Emory's loss will be the gain of some
more fortunate city. Victor is a power where ever he may be." He relocated to Myrtle Springs in adjacent Van Zandt County.

Apparently, Rose left Emory because he had alienated merchants
in town by siding with area farmers. This is an example of his turn to
populism and polemicism after the war. In his December letter to Guy
Bryan, W. P. Zuber wrote:

> While he was sending me his "Star," I gathered from his editorials that
> he was growing unpopular in the town of Emory. In one of the last
> that I read, he said that an erroneous impression had become prev-
> alent that he was laboring to prejudice the country people of Rains
> County against the people of the town. This he said was a mistake. He
> explained that the merchants of Emory sold their goods too high, and
> paid too little for produce: and that he had only directed the atten-
> tion of the merchants to this fact; advised them to sell goods cheaper,
> and pay more for cotton and wool; and admonished them that, unless
> they should do so, the farmers of the county would drop them, and
> trade elsewhere. Whether his councels [sic] were sound or otherwise,
> the evidence was that, with the merchants at least, he was growingly
> unpopular. This on his own explanation.[12]

Another point of friction might have been Rose's lack of support for
James S. Hogg's candidacy for governor, putting him out of step with
the sentiment in Rains County, where voters, by a margin of 590 to 157,
had overwhelmingly chosen Hogg over his two opponents in the recent
gubernatorial election.[13] Yet Rose was his own man. He once wrote to
John Henry Brown, "Independence is, perhaps, my most marke[d] trait
of character, and, like Ben Harrison, I try to please myself. I value more
the approval of conscience than the applause of crowds."[14]

The *Star*'s new location in Myrtle Springs was announced in the *Fort
Worth Gazette* in its issue of May 24, 1891: "The plant of the Emory
Star has been removed to Myrtle Springs. It is in charge of Mr. Victor

M. Rose, and he will begin the publication of a paper at that point in a few days." Rose renamed the weekly the *Herald*, only two issues of which have survived—from August and November 1891. Unlike other newspapers that Rose edited, the *Myrtle Springs Herald* sported a masthead giving a company name, the Myrtle Springs Publishing Company, as editor and publisher rather than Rose himself.

Myrtle Springs was likely an attractive location to Rose because the recently organized Myrtle Springs Investment Company was heavily promoting the new town, which was still being platted in 1891. With signs of being the area's next boomtown, Myrtle Springs was a place where Rose could write the kind of promotional articles that had filled the pages of *The Old Capitol*. By championing the town in his paper, Rose perhaps hoped to find a warm, appreciative reception from the community.

Yet during his time at Myrtle Springs, Rose apparently voiced opinions that riled others. A February 29, 1892, issue of the *Dallas Morning News*, is highly critical of Rose:

Victor Rose of the *Myrtle Springs Herald* crows like Tam O'Shanter[15] when o'er all the ills of life victorious

Factories make towns. Myrtle has the factories and will have more, consequently Myrtle is to be the town. The paper mill is as sure as a nickel in the slot—so Mr. Dorge assures us. The paper mill will consume all your wheat and rye straw, broom-corn stalk, etc., thus widening the margin for profits to the producer. The Myrtle Springs factory will soon be turning out new brooms in quantities to appease the most insatiate wholesale dealers. The canning factory will hold the boards when the fruit comes in. We have the coal right at hand when we need it. The salt wells will be panning out 500 barrels against the completion of the railroad to Myrtle. Vitrified brick are on the bills. Myrtle will soon be furnishing a considerable per cent of the paper supply to the southwest. Myrtle had red ochre enough to paint forty-nine stripes around the globe. It is panning out jimdandy, both as to quantity and quality. The college can take care of itself henceforth. It has passed its minority. Healing waters free. The sweet

singers of Myrtle are making progress. Hominy as well harmony. The
ferro-manganese water is the best tonic known. The "spouting glory"
and the spring nearest the pavilion are ferro-maganese.

If Chapman had been Rose there would have been no occasion to
tell him to crow.[16]

Despite the criticisms faced by Rose in his new home, both surviving
issues of the *Myrtle Springs Herald* contain two lengthy articles about the
benefits of Myrtle Springs. One, titled "Plateau City of Texas: Prospects
Galore—Health, Happiness and Wealth—All at Myrtle Springs," gives
a general description of the town's agricultural and industrial features,
especially its mineral springs. The other, headlined "Ho! For Van Zandt
County! The Immigrant's Paradise—Join Us and Prosper with the Prosperous," provides positive statistical information. Both issues of the paper
contain testimonials from individuals who make bold claims for the
curative properties of the springs.

The paper must have been in circulation by early June 1891, as the
Galveston Daily News of June 7 mentions that the *Myrtle Springs Herald*
had praised the agricultural coverage of the *Galveston-Dallas News*, and
endlessly lauds the healing properties of the chalybeate waters. There
was virtually no malady that the sulfurous water could not cure. Described as having been designed by the "Supreme Architect," healing is
assured with every draught, and all for free.

In 1891, Rose makes a sly notice to the fact that Cherokees were
getting $17,000 per capita. This made them the "wealthiest people on
earth."[17] Victor continued to release articles and produce for the *Myrtle
Springs Herald*, until tragedy struck the Rose family.

By the end of 1891, Victor received the news that his mother had
died of coronary disease on October 21, 1891, in Kelly, New Mexico.
Her last words were "I am going to faint."[18] After leaving Victoria for
Llano County in 1879, Margaret Rose had moved to Baylor County
and then Wilbarger County in northwestern Texas in 1884, and then
to New Mexico in 1886, following her youngest sons, John Washington
Rose and Preston Robinson Rose, and their families.[19] The *Victoria*

Advocate announced her death on October 31: "Mrs. Rose, wife of Judge J.H. [*sic*] Rose, a former citizen of Victoria, died at Kelly, New Mexico, a few days ago. Mrs. Rose was the mother of Mrs. G.O. Stoner and Messrs. Victor and Volney Rose."

In early 1889, unaware that his mother and two brothers had left Texas by this time and moved to New Mexico, Rose wrote the following postscript in a letter to John Henry Brown: "My mother, with her two younger sons, are at Seymour, Baylor Co.; and my aunt at C'oncho. They are broken up as to property. I have seen none of my family, save my brother Volney, and sister, Mrs. G.O. Stoner, both at Victoria, for years."[20] Presumably he had not seen his daughter, either. In the same month that Margaret Rose died, Julia Rose Anderson became seriously ill with typhoid fever, but recovered.[21] It is not known why Victor was so alienated from his family, unless it was due to his newfound political stance and numerous scandals.

Rose was nearing the age of fifty and may have grown weary of the relentless grind of newspaper publishing, or his health may have been in decline. The *Brenham Daily Banner* of August 3, 1892, contained the one-sentence announcement that "Victor M. Rose has retired from the editorship of the Myrtle Springs Herald."

Victor Marion Rose died in Myrtle Springs on January 21, 1893—at two o'clock in the morning.[22] According to Kathryn Stoner O'Connor, pneumonia was the cause of death, but Victor's sister Zilpa recounted a more dramatic passing: "He ... died from the wound he received in the Civil War, a bullet went into his face in the cheek and lodged behind his ear. Finally the doctor said it reached the brain and killed him. He was buried ... without a relative to mourn for him."[23]

The *Times* obituary summarized Rose's Civil War service and published books, and then added that he had written "a great many newspaper articles of historical value." It also noted that Rose was "well known to every old-timer in the county." The *Brownsville Herald* of January 26, 1893, called Rose "a pioneer printer in Southwest Texas" and added, "Many are the friends who will regret his death." Like the *Victoria Times*, the *Victoria Advocate* printed a detailed obituary:

The deceased was a native of Victoria, having been born there in the year 1843 [sic]. We are indebted to his untiring energy in the search for data and statistics, and his love for history, for that valuable work called "Victoria County, Texas—Its Settlement, Development and Its Progress." Victor Marion Rose was the eldest son of Judge John W. Rose, and the brother of Volney J. Rose and Mrs. G.O. Stoner. His father was one of our largest land and slave owners before the war, and lavishly bestowed upon Victor the benefits of a higher university education, which the young man took every advantage of until the war between the states commenced, when he enlisted in the confederate army and was a valiant soldier. For a while after the war he served on the editorial staff of the Advocate.[24]

Victor Rose continued to be remembered in Victoria, and the *Advocate* kept up with the activities of his only child, Julia Rosa Rose Anderson, who made frequent trips from Thomaston to Victoria to visit her aunt, Nellie Borland Wood (later Kriesle). After a 1907 visit, the *Advocate* reported: "Mrs. R.W. Anderson . . . returned on the evening train to Thomaston. Her father was editor of the Advocate several years. He also published a Laredo paper and the Capitol at an early date. Mrs. Anderson kindly offered to lend us some of his papers bound in a volume from which we expect to gather a great deal of South Texas history for the enjoyment of our readers."[25] Victor must have regularly sent Julia copies of his newspapers.

A few references to the *Myrtle Springs Herald* are found in issues of the state press from 1894 and 1895, evidence that another editor took over the paper after Rose's death. However, the name of his successor is not known.

Victor had devoted his entire writing career—in his historical works and in many of his poems—to paying tribute to others. In 1936, the year of the Texas Centennial, he himself was honored with a place in history with a monument erected at his gravesite in Evergreen Cemetery in Victoria. The inscription reads as follows:

VICTOR MARION ROSE
Poet, Editor, Historian and Soldier
From the Founders of Victoria
He Gathered the Fragments of the
Past and Wove them into the
History of Victoria County

The inscription also gives birth and death details (the dates are unfortunately incorrect). Another Centennial project, a marker commemorating the *Victoria Advocate* as the state's second-oldest newspaper, honored Victor by including his name on the plaque as one of its editors.

Well into the twentieth century, Victoria continued to honor this native son. In 1965, at Courthouse Square in Victoria, a Texas Historical Marker was erected to commemorate Victor as a "Noted Texas Newspaper Man and Author," with a lengthy inscription that included the titles of his historical works. And in 1989 Victor's name again appeared on a Texas Historical Marker erected at the site of the *Advocate's* offices to commemorate the paper's long history.

Some of Rose's works, after being reprinted in the twentieth century, are becoming available as ebooks and thus accessible to a wider audience. This is very fitting for a writer like Rose since, along with his intense interest in the past, he was also forward-looking, and he often expressed excitement about the course of progress and the possibilities of the future. Although he could not have foreseen the advances of twenty-first-century technology, "ye old pencil pusher" would surely have welcomed them. His legacy lives on.

EPILOGUE

DURING the course of my research, I have arrived at a great appreciation for Victor's writing. His remarkable range left me mildly thunderstruck, as I had always thought of him as a "fluff" writer, never having recovered from the days of the Old South. This has been proven to be so untrue.

His writing is powerful, lucid, and interesting. His recovery from the fantasy of the Old South was unusual and courageous. Throughout his correspondence, where we really get to know him, we see a man of strong convictions and courage—one who takes his research and work seriously. Clearly, Victor had evolved well beyond being the so-called pampered "sissy" of his earlier years.

Victor spent much of his life paying tribute to others. Finally, in 1936, he was honored with a place in history. His remains were returned to Victoria and rest in Evergreen Cemetery with a monument that reminds us, "He gathered the fragments of the past and wove them into the history of Victoria County."

Yet he did much more than just that. Victor Marion Rose left us with works on many subjects, and much could have been lost to history had he not written it all down. Even more important is the fact that he was a firsthand witness to much of his subject matter. This recognition would have gratified Victor, no doubt, as he was placed in the select group of historical figures honored during the Texas Centenary, an event that would have filled him with pride and enthusiasm, and perhaps have inspired many articles and poems from his "faber." As late as 1965 and 1989 in Victoria at the *Advocate* and around the courthouse square, he was being honored as a notable Texas writer. He once acclaimed in

"Victoria Regina"[1] that he was "Home again with his wanderer's heart." So now he is at rest in his native home, a place he once shocked and scandalized.

Along with his intense interest in the past, he was also forward-looking and often expressed excitement about the course of the future. Sadly, he was to die far too young.

While not overlooking his often "bad boy" behavior and alcoholism, after this study of the literary side of my ancestor, I am proud to call him "Uncle Vic."

APPENDIX ONE

The Brookings Family

IN AN ARTICLE in *True West* magazine from June 1976, we find a thorough history of the Brookings family. According to this article, there are a number of escapades associated with this family that could explain some of the consternation felt by Victor Rose's family concerning his marriage to Ada Brookings.

There are suggestions of horse thieving by Bood Brookings, and when brought to trial, it appears that someone lied in court for him and he went free. Bood and his brother, Bill, were described as characters, performing all types of dangerous and crazy capers, such as cornering a panther in a cave and smoking him out to kill him. Legend also has it that the brothers got in several intense arguments—one time as to when the sun would set. Bood also had a dog that would rustle cattle for him. The two brothers were involved in the Sutton-Taylor feud and were free range men who didn't like fencing. Bood engaged in several scrapes in his time, many relating to the Sutton-Taylor feud. Eventually they moved to more open country in Arizona and New Mexico.

Margaret Rose married Robert Pitts Brooking, and this began the connection between the Rose and Brookings families. Julia Rose Brookings, who later married Needham, was the cousin of Julia Rosa Rose, Victor Rose's daughter. Apparently, Julia Rosa Rose was enchanted with Julia Brookings and would sit for hours under an apple tree rocking her. Later, they never saw each other again, but were pen pals forever. Ada, Victor's second marriage, was a sister of Julia Needham's father, Robert P. Brookings. One of the uncles, Upshire Brookings, was a gambler.

As noted, the Brookings men were involved in the Sutton-Taylor feud for years. Bill Brookings was a drifter, a "rolling stone"—apparently, the entire family was less than well regarded. Julia Needham's parents were divorced, not a thing well thought of in those days. At one time, her father was hunted by the later Dalton gang, possibly because he had forbidden her to go to a party with one of the gang members. Her mother eventually went to New Mexico where their uncle, Preston Rose, was at the time. Even her marriage to Needham made for a hard scrabble life for her. From semioutlaws to subsistence farmers, it is possible to see why the Brookings family was not well liked or considered socially equal to the Southern planter class of Victoria.

APPENDIX TWO

Henry Eustace McCulloch

A Biographical Sketch

AS PRINTED in the *Myrtle Springs Herald*, November 19, 1891:

[continued from last week]

Henry McCulloch, at the head of a detachment of his own men, and gallant old Mr. Thurmond, with a like number of Cameron's company, pushing on to the town of Mier, and after learning the exact situation of affairs returned, just as Canalles, at the head of 500 cavalry was entering the town; and reported to Col. Fisher that Ampudia was also advancing upon the same point; and advised him to defeat the cavalry before the infantry and artillery under Ampudia arrived; which he failed to do, with the sad result already enumerated —McCulloch, with rare sagacity, reading in the too apparent lack of the necessary qualities for command which characterised the movements of the head of the Texian force, determined to extricate his command from the net which was being spun by the hands of Fate for their discomfiture, and struck out for home, through an uninhabited country, and without an ounce of bread and meat. A fat young mustang mare was shot and killed, which, after a fast of three days was voted luscious food by the men. Henry McCulloch finally reached home, to learn that he was the father of a daughter three weeks old; and that his friends had placed him in nomination for the office of sheriff, to which position he was elected by a very handsome majority. But the times were "hard," there being no money in circulation, and at the end of his term he discovered that his services, at his own expense, had well nigh bankrupted him; and but for the timely assistance of his friend, Capt. Isaac N. Mitchell, who *forced* him to accept a loan of one thousand dollars, must have commenced the struggle of life anew. With this aid he purchased a stock of goods, and in a short time was enabled to return the capital, and continue his business operations;—removing his family and store, in November 1845 to the town of Seguin as a more healthy section; and remained in the mercantile business until the year 1849; in the interim serving through the Mexican war, as captain of a company of Rangers. Reporting for duty to Col. W.S. Harney, at San Antonio, he was instructed to establish a camp upon the head waters of the San Marcos, and guard that frontier from the incursions of the savages, and reached the designated post June 12, 1846. The company guarded an immense wagon train from San Antonio to Monclova, Mo., in charge of Capt. Newton, A.Q.M. of the regular army, loaded with clothing and specie for the use of the American army; and in his report to Gen. Wool, Capt. Newton said: "I was never with a company in the regular service which maintained better discipline; their conduct was both gentlemanly and soldierly; every duty was performed promptly and efficiently, and without the least trouble or annoyance to their captain, whom they seem to obey more through love than fear. As an officer he is strict, and as a man so kind that every man in the company seems to feel perfectly easy in his presence." General Wool also compliment[ed] the captain upon the soldierly appearance of his company; and it was generally believed that he was by no means an admirer of "Citizen Soldiery," because of their want of discipline. In the autumn of 1840 Col. P. Handsboro Bell was assigned by the governor to the command of all the Rangers on the Texas frontier; and a bat[t]alion, under Major Tom T. Smith, was organised of the companies of McCulloch, Grumbles, S.P. Ross, and Highsmith; which were stationed at proper points to guard the settlements from Indian depredations; that of McCulloch being posted in Hamilton's Valley.

This service continued until December 1848, when the dragoons superseded the Rangers; during which period the company had re-enlisted four times; and Henry E. McCulloch as often chosen to the command by the free suffrages of his comrades. During the later year of service on the frontier Captain McCulloch had his family with him, quartered in a comfortable log house; and *en route* home, Mrs.

McCulloch became quite sick in Austin; which influenced him to become the proprietor of the Swisher House, which inn he kept until the year 1850; closing out his business in Seguin. At the urgent request of Gen. Brook, U.S.A. commanding at San Antonio, he raised a company of Rangers in the year last named, for service on the lower Nueces, Aransas, and Mission rivers; the Indians having become so bold that many of the inhabitants were abandoning their homes.

Taking position on the Aransas river, about three miles above the Goliad and San Patricio road, he succeeded, after a number of skirmishes and close pursuits, in closing that section to the ingress of the savages, until immigration had rendered the citizens so numerous as to preclude any fear in the future from that quarter. The company was then—1851,—transferred to the Llano river, accompanied by Captain Joseph E. Johnston, of the topographical engineers, and established camp near the present locality of Junction city, on the North Fork of the Llano. He soon struck an Indian trail, and surprised a party of some 30 warriors and two squaws, both of whom fought with great earnestness, until captured and disarmed. A number of Comanches were killed, and the remainder dispersed. The squaws were released, having been given sufficient food to subsist upon until able to reach their own people.

The company was mustered out of the service by Capt. James Longstreet, at Fort Martin Scott, on November 4, 1857, which concluded H.E. McCulloch's military services under the U.S. government. In 1853 he became the candidate of the democratic party for a seat in the legislature, his competitor being Col. French Smith; and delivered his maiden stump speech to the "sovereigns" at Seguin, in reply to a "rattling good appeal of Col. Smith in behalf of the whig party; and as he left the stand amid the cheers of all; his opponent, congratulating him, said: "Well, Mac, I knew you could fight like h—ll; but had no idea you could make such a speech. But I'll wallop you at the polls!" But the colonel rec[k]oned without his host, as McCulloch was chosen to a seat in the legislature by a handsome majority. At the expiration of his term in the lower house, he was elected a member of the state senate; and served two consecutive sessions in that body; when Ben McCulloch resigning the marshalship for the eastern district, he received the appointment from President Buchanan, May 7, 1859. Being satisfied the state would secede, and wishing to have as little, or no funds of government in his possession as possible, in that event he opened the December term of the court for 1860 with but $5,000 on hand; and although the judge was informed of this, and the further fact that the requisitions of southern marshals were not being honored, the court was continued in session until the whole of the above amount was exhausted; and the marshal was compelled to advance the necessary means to the amount of $2,000, for the payment of jurors, witnesses, bailiffs' and imperative charges.* The secession convention, on the 5th day of February 1861 appointed Ben McCulloch, Henry E. McCulloch, and John S. Ford, colonels of cavalry, charged with receiving the surrender of the U.S. forts in the state; and the McCulloch brothers repaired to their home near Seguin to make the necessary arrangements, and departed—Ben for San Antonio, and Henry for the line of posts on the north-west frontier—never to meet more upon earth. The latter hastened to his purposed field of operations; collected quite a volunteer force; and succeeded in reaching the neighborhood of Camp Colorado unobserved; when, as a traveler, he called at the quarters of the commandant, Captain E. Kirby Smith, and before making known his mission, engaged the officers of the post in conversation; during the course of which he learned that they were all southern men; and that while they would undoubtedly act with the south when they deemed the proper time had arrived, they felt a professional pride which would stipulate for honor to the flag, and the transfer of the troopers, with their arms and accoutrements to some place under authority of the Federal government. Finally he announced his mission, and after much hesitancy, Capt. Smith agreed to surrender the public property; men to march out with flying colors, transportation to be furnished them to Indianola, where he purposed taking ship for some northern port. Early the next morning the mail arrived, bringing intelligence of Gen. Twigg's surrender at San Antonio; it also brought Captain Smith his commission as a Major. Having captured Ft. Chodum [?], and Camp Cook, complying with all the instructions of the convention, he returned to the state capital, where he found a colonel's commission awaiting him, from the provisional president of the Confederate states, with authority to organise a Texas regiment of cavalry for that service, upon the western frontier of the state. The regiment was composed of the companies of: Captains Fry;

W.A. Pitts; M.M. Boggess; Goveneur Nelson; P. Hill Ashby; W.G. Tobin; Buck Barry; T.C. Frost;———Webb; and———Davidson. Col. McCulloch received, as the commanding Confederate officer in Texas, transfer from the state of the arms and munitions of war lately surrendered; and caused an artillery company to be organised, and equipped; of which Wm. Edgar was appointed captain; as well as assimilating otherwise the chaotic elements of the two services into order, and a state of efficiency.

*NOTE: After the conclusion of the war between the States General McCulloch, together with his sureties, was sued in the U.S. District court at Galveston, for a considerable sum alleged to have been due the government on account of his expenditures as marshal; and notwithstanding the fact that he introduced positive testimony showing that he was entitled to receive, for funds advanced, and commissions for taking the census of 1860, some $2,500, judgment was rendered against him; and though he succeeded, by compromise, through the influence of republican friends in having the amount reduced, was compelled to make an unjust payment; which, by reason of his reduced pecuniary circumstances, was severely felt.

—*Myrtle Springs Herald*, November 19, 1891

A Selection of Poems by Victor Marion Rose

In the 1960s, Victor Marion Rose's niece, Kathryn Stoner O'Connor, helped restore the venerable mission that is the subject of the following poem.

La Bahia
By Wild Rose

Oh La Bahia! in grandeur hoary
Thy ruined old bastions rise,
Thy walls, bright with historic glory
Still gleam 'gainst the blue of the skies!

Here were brave, true hearts doomed to languish,
Chilled by the fierce breath of despair,
These rocks caught the last wail of anguish
And echoed the last low-breathed prayer.

Dark clouds rising to the blue zenith,
In morning's smile blush warm and red;
Shadows flee; flowers and sun-light mingle
Above the green mound of the dead.

The river so silently creeping
Along where low lieth their dust,
Makes verdant the sod that is keeping
The martyr's loved ashes in trust.

Methinks in the full flush of battle
'Twere grand to die! when loud and clear
Vict'rys cheer, cannon's roar, and the rattle
Of musketry quickens the ear!

But, ah! 'twas the acme of valor
When calm, 'mid the carnage of blood,
Where all was lost, save their own honor
The heroes of old La Bahia stood.

When bravely the noble souled Fannin,
Disdaining a suppliant's part,
Unfalteringly gave the last signal
That sped the ball to his own heart.

Oh wife, in love's vision of beauty,
Looking out toward our star circled zone,
Did you dream the proud sense of duty
That called him away from love's own—

The thrill of heroic emotion,
That kindled the warrior's breath—
The liberty child's pure devotion
Would be quenched in the chalice of death?

Was the hope in your bosom burning
That soon in fame's bright annals known,
The conquering hero returning
Should clasp you, and call you his own?

Oh did your heart break with sobbing;
Though your fond eyes ne'er could bedew
The token he sent, his heart throbbing
Its last thought for home and for you.

Did gleam from the glory light shining
Far down the dim vista of years,
Show laurel wreath's 'round his name twining
Begemmed with a people's warm tear?

Oblivious of the world's praises,
Where sweet Southern summer still keeps
Her vigil; 'neath white waving daisies
The stern hearted warrior sleeps.

Oh Georgia, the sound of thy weeping,
Thy sorrow, thy anguish, thy pain
Have passed; here thy loved ones are sleeping
But the holocaust was not in vain.

For peace holds her gentle dominion
On mountain, hill, valley and wave,
And liberty spreads her bright pinion
O'er the land bought with blood of thy brave.

But where is the monument showing
Our love for the heroes who fought,
With the gift of whose life blood out pouring
Our emblem of freedom was wrought?

Shall gratitude's rich, full oblation,
Return in warm life giving showers?
Or pity, and faint approbation
Fall chill on fair chivalry's flowers?

O land, by their hearts once compassioned
Whose glory now shines o'er the seas,
Whose warm Southern clime seems but fashioned
By nature, when anxious to please.

Beauty's home, where she ever lingers
Bestowing her gifts with free hand;
Shall in gratitude's grimy fingers
Stain thy fame, oh, beautiful land.

The Alamo hath its proud columns
Inscribed with bright immortal names;
As noble a commemoration
The blood-imbrued La Bahia claims!

The while there is one true heart beating
That thrills at the name of the brave,
Rest not, till fair liberty's greeting
Rises o'er valor's long unmarked grave!

—*Victoria Advocate*, February 14, 1880

In "Perdu," Rose continues to take note of his annoyance with prudish convention. This is the demon that he lets us see from time to time.

Perdu
January, 1864

I
Madoña, list to thy lover's lay,
Which breathes in tones of sadness low,
A wretched heart's deep freight of woe!
List, Madoña, to thy lover's lay!

II
But not for me, alas, those classic charms,
That nameless spell that holds me bound,
To thy sweet voice's merest sound,
Though in another's arms.

III
For *him*, O may thy plighted vows remain!
Nor would I e'er (may God forefend
To shield the sacred name of friend)—
Cause him dishonor's cruel pain.

IV
But be it ours alone, O fatal sweet!
My heart's bright idol and another's wife,
The cold convention of a formal life,
And crush our very hearts whene'er we meet.

V

Thou knowest not, nor ever shalt thou know,
The impious legend writ my restive soul above,
In ink shed by my heart to lawless love,
And consecrate to misery and woe.

VI

My song dies on the evening's fitful breeze,
My blasted hopes, to feed upon themselves retire,
And herd with worms, where once Promethean fire
Sparkled like ruby wine above the lees.

NOTE. This expression of a morbid, not to say vicious sentiment, would have been eliminated from the present collection, had not the author allowed his inclinations to be overruled by the counsels of some friends. Of the three personalities adverted to in the verses, the author is the survivor; and while he would attempt no defense for such figurative moral obliquity, he feels sure that it is not more depraved than many emanations from the highly aesthetical regions of the modern Parnassus. Besides, poetry is the prose of nature, and it is true just in proportion to its fidelity to nature. The perfect characters drawn in compliance with the demands of a prudish conventionality, have no place in human nature; and though we may write ourselves as saints ever so often, we may not in truth raise our natures much above the carnal desires of poor, fallen man.

A true acrostic is a poem in which the initial letters of each level form a word—in this case "Garfield." James Abram Garfield was the twentieth president of the United States who was shot July 2, 1881.

Garfield
An Acrostic

Garfield, a nation mourns thy death—its loss,
And Christians kneel beneath the heavy cross,
Raised now in hovel and palatial hall;
For opposition, at thy cruel fall,
Inspired by pure and patriotic breath,
Entombed for aye the party Shibboleth.

Living, Philanthropy enriched thy name!
Dying, thou hast bequeathed it all to fame!

***

Rose wrote of friendship and regard for others he admired in "Demara, the Comanche Queen."

Demara, the Comanche Queen

EXPLANATORY

While composing these verses, I frequently thought of George W. Pascal, the brave and generous friend of my boyhood, in whose veins coursed the proudest of aboriginal blood. He won renown on distant fields, as a Ranger, in combats with the Comanches and Apaches, and later, as lieutenant-colonel of the 1st Texas (Union) cavalry.

And though I followed the *ignis fatuus* of a vain delusion under the "Stars and Bars," I never suffered the embers on the altar of friendship to grow cold; and if these lines should meet his eye, it will afford me increased satisfaction to know that he has received this assurance of my undiminished regard and friendship.

***

The "Song of June" was printed in Sam H. Dixon's *The Poets and Poetry of Texas*,[1] showing Rose's stature as a writer and literary figure in his time. The first five verses show us his redressing of the losses and sorrows of war.

Song of June

I
Speed, Mercury, speed to the court of each god,
And summon the children of light;
O'er Samos, and Argos, sacred each sod,
To Olympia on with thy flight!

II

On the top of Olympus the feast shall be spread,
On the heaven's etherial brink;
Be ambrosia to-night, immortals, our bread;
And the nectar of gods our drink!

III

At their nuptials this eve let the pandean pipe
Sound sweetly of love and of fire;
Bid Orpheus come with his fame full and ripe,
Eurydice will list to his lyre.

IV

O welcome the brave young patriot now,
And Livia fair at his side—
And this hero's wreath, O place on his brow,
And this crown shall be for his bride.

V

Now little it recks the colors he bore,
Or the side that he took in the fray,
For the tocsin of war shall summon no more,
To battle the blue and the gray.

Timeline and Newspaper Career of Victor Marion Rose

NOTE: An anthology of Rose's works are available on The Texas Coastal Bend website: www.texascoastalbend.org.

1846—Annexation and the Mexican-American War (took place when Rose was a toddler)

1848—Treaty of Guadalupe-Hidalgo

1853—Railroad construction

}   Happenings in Rose's youth

1854—First telegraph office in the United States

1860–1865—Civil War

1865—Emancipation

}   Rose participated in the war and also had a strong opinion on the way emancipation was carried out.

1869—First African American in Texas legislature (One could connect this to Rose's *Old Capitol* writings about blacks who were achieving after Emancipation.)

1873—Buffalo soldiers in Texas

1876—Texas adopted the Constitution of 1876, complied with public opinion, but there is no record of Rose making a comment on this (see https://tshaonline.org/handbook/online/articles/mhc07).

1882—Women's equality—early days—connect to Rose's changing about women and suffrage, irrespective of race, color, or sex.

1888—New capitol completed—Rose's political times

1891—Railroad Commission established—James Hogg, the governor of Texas in the 1890s, was determined to establish a Railroad Commission. Rose was vehemently against James Hogg.

1893—Texas Equal Rights Association formed—The year of Rose's death

1894—Oil discovered in Corsicana—Had this happened thirty years earlier in the Coastal Bend, the Rose family plantation may have been saved.

Rose's Newspaper Career

Rose's newspaper jobs were extensive. He worked with the following newspapers:

Victoria Advocate—Victoria, Texas—1869 to 1873 (Coeditor and publisher)

Laredo Times—Laredo, Texas—1884 to 1886 (Editor and publisher)

The Old Capitol—Columbia, Texas—1887 to 1889

The Emory Star—Emory, Texas—1890 to 1892

Myrtle Springs Herald—Myrtle Springs, Texas—1892

Galveston Daily News (This paper picked up many of Rose's stories from around the state.)

The Brazos Pilot (Rose worked for this paper—articles appeared in the Galveston paper.)

The Evening Light—San Antonio, Texas

Two Republics

Liberal Mexican Press

Pilot (Rose worked for this paper—articles appeared in the Galveston paper.)

The Evening Light—San Antonio, Texas

Two Republics

Liberal Mexican Press

NOTES

Foreword: An Introduction to "Uncle Vic"

1. This foreword was compiled from interviews with Margaret Stoner McLean by Louise S. O'Connor, September 7, 1997, and November 7, 2002, Georgetown, Texas.

2. Mame Stoner married Thomas Royal Stoner, a distant cousin; hence her name appears as Mame Stoner Stoner.

3. Anna Wellington Stoner's son, Thomas Royal Stoner, married Victor's niece, Mamie Victoria Stoner, daughter of Zilpa Rose and George Overton Stoner. The following is an example of her writing: "The water in the creek those mornings was nearly milk warm and a steam rose from it like your breath on a cold day." Lois Myers, *Letters by Lamplight* (Waco: Baylor University Press, 1991), 113.

4. He published *The Texas Vendetta; Or, The Sutton-Taylor Feud* (1880); *Ross' Texas Brigade* (1881); *Some Historical Facts in Regard to the Settlement of Victoria, Texas: Its Progress and Present Status* (1883; reprinted in 1961 as *A Republication of the Book Most Often Known as Victor Rose's* History of Victoria), which he dedicated to John J. Linn; and *The Life and Services of Gen. Ben McCulloch* (1888). Craig H. Roell, "Rose, Victor Marion," *Handbook of Texas Online*, accessed April 27, 2017, http://www.tshaonline.org/handbook/online/articles/fro73.

Introduction

1. "Literature of the Antebellum South—Richard Gray (Essay Date 1986)," *Nineteenth-Century Literary Criticism*, vol. 112, ed. Lynn M. Zott (Farmington Hills, MI: Gale Cengage, 2002), accessed August 19, 2013, http://www.enotes.com/literature-antebellum-south-essays/literature-antebellum-south/richard-gray-essay-date-1986.

2. Carl N. Deglers, "The Foundation of Southern Distinctiveness," *The Southern Review* 13, no. 2 (April 1977): 225–39. An understanding of the Old South and its ways gives a better context for Victor Rose and his writings.

3. W. J. Cash, *The Mind of the South* (New York: Vintage Books, 1991), xlix.

4. "Literature of the Antebellum South—Introduction," *Nineteenth-Century Literary Criticism*, vol. 112, ed. Lynn M. Zott (Farmington Hills, MI: Gale Cengage,

2002), accessed January 11, 2017, http://www.enotes.com/topics/literature-antebellum-south#critical-essays-literature-antebellum-south-introduction.

5. "Literature of the Antebellum South—Jan Bakker (Essay Date 1986)," *Nineteenth- Century Literary Criticism*, vol. 112, ed. Lynn M. Zott (Farmington Hills, MI: Gale Cengage, 2002), accessed September 16, 2012, http://www.enotes.com/literature-antebellum-south-criticism/literature-antebellum-south/jan-bakker-essay-date-1986.

6. Deglers, "The Foundation of Southern Distinctiveness," 225–39.

7. Hon. Robert Mercer Taliaferro Hunter, "Origin of the Late War," *Southern Historical Society Papers*, I, January (1876), 5, accessed August 19, 2013, http://www.civilwarhome.com/warorigin.htm.

8. "Literature of the Antebellum South—C. Alphonso Smith (Essay Date 1908)," *Nineteenth-Century Literary Criticism*, vol. 112, ed. Lynn M. Zott (Farmington Hills, MI: Gale Cengage, 2002), accessed August 19, 2013, http://www.enotes.com/literature-antebellum-south-essays/literature-antebellum-south/c-alphonso-smith-essay-date-1908.

9. Victor M. Rose, *Ross' Texas Brigade: Being a Narrative of Events Connected with Its Service in the Late War between the States* (Louisville: Courier-Journal Company, 1881), 141.

10. Cash, *The Mind of the South*. See also *Catalogue of the Officers and Students in Centenary College of Louisiana, 1859–60* (Baton Rouge: Daily Advocate, n.d.), xviii.

11. As indicated in the acceptance speech of the Queen of Love and Beauty, Margaret McLean, quoted in "Tournaments: An Account of This Early Sport in Victoria, Texas and Neighboring Communities," *The Cattleman*, September 1, 1948.

12. Victor M. Rose, *Demara, the Comanche Queen; and Other Rhymes* (New York: J. J. Little & Co., 1882), 13.

13. Brett and Kate McKay, "Manly Honor Part V: Honor in the American South," accessed November 26, 2012; http://www.artofmanliness.com.

14. "Philip Pendleton Cooke (1816–50), Contributed by William Bland Whitley and the *Dictionary of Virginia Biography*," Encyclopedia Virginia, accessed December 11, 2017, http://www.encyclopediavirginia.org/Cooke_Philip_Pendleton_1816-1850: "Philip Pendleton Cooke was a poet whose work emphasized lost love, the natural world, and exoticism, placing him firmly within the romantic literary movement. Cooke practiced law in western Virginia but struggled to make a living at writing. His association with Edgar Allan Poe led to the publication of his most famous work, the poem 'Florence Vane' (1840), which continues to be anthologized as an example of romantic poetry."

15. Robert E. Lee adhered to an honor code that made him stay loyal to the South.

16. McKay, "Manly Honor Part V: Honor in the American South."

17. "Kemper Kernals," *Victoria Advocate*, March 13, 1880.

18. "Literature of the Antebellum South—Thomas Nelson Page (Essay Date 1892)," *Nineteenth-Century Literary Criticism*, vol. 112, ed. Lynn M. Zott

(Farmington Hills, MI: Gale Cengage, 2002), accessed October 8, 2012, http://www.enotes.com/literature-antebellum-south-essays/literature-antebellum-south/thomas-nelson-page-essay-date-1892.

19. Jesus F. de la Teja, *Lone Star Unionism, Dissent, and Resistance: Other Sides of Civil War Texas* (Norman: University of Oklahoma Press, 2016), 19.

20. *The Old Capitol*, November 17, 1888, p. 2, col. 3.

21. This information came from family legend and genealogy.

22. His inheritance would have been a large plantation, a very comfortable income, and the ability to write without the need to earn a living.

23. Few European immigrants at this time came to the South to work for two reasons: (1) because manufacturing jobs were more profitable for them and (2) possibly because they were fleeing aristocratic oppression in Europe. There just was no middle class place in Southern culture, either. The concept of "white trash" is of interest to understanding the caste system of the South.

The definition of "white trash" in the South is a class firmly situated in between the aristocratic planters and the slaves. They could never be elevated, not even economically. They were considered human waste and could in no way uplift themselves. They were a lower class than slaves. In the Southern mind, blacks could be uplifted, but "white trash" was irretrievable and a distinct class. When they became symbols of partisan politics, this is where they became of interest in the South. The women were considered sluts living in filthy cabins, lacking manners and engaged in rampant breeding. Passing on horrific traits, they were never able to improve and were the mark of evolutionary decline. They were considered a danger to the integrity of the South. See Nancy Isenberg, *White Trash: The 400-Year Untold History of Class in America* (New York: Viking, 2016).

24. Interview with Alene Pettus Lott by Louise S. O'Connor, January 10, 1992.

25. Cash, *The Mind of the South*, 99–104.

26. J. W. Petty Jr., ed., *A Republishing of the Book Most Often Known as Victor Rose's* History of Victoria (Victoria, TX: Book Mart, 1961), 74.

27. Ibid, 43.

28. Interview with Margaret Stoner McLean, Georgetown, Texas, by Louise O'Connor, September 4, 1997.

29. Rose, *Ross' Texas Brigade*, 170.

30. Ibid., 35.

31. Ibid., 138.

32. Ibid., 135.

33. Don B. Graham, "Texas Historical Literature," accessed August 19, 2013, http://www.freepages.family.rootsweb.ancestry.com/~families/briscoe/txhistory.html.

34. *The Old Capitol*, November 17, 1888, p. 2, col. 1.

35. *The Old Capitol*, November 24, 1888.

36. Carl H. Moneyhon, *Texas after the Civil War: The Struggle of Reconstruction* (College Station: Texas A&M University Press, 2004).

37. Defined as an incurable urge to write.

38. Rose, *Demara*, 5.

39. Gregg Cantrell, *Stephen F. Austin: Empresario of Texas* (New Haven and London: Yale University Press, 1999), 373; Robert M. Utley, *Lone Star Justice, The First Century of the Texas Rangers* (Oxford and New York: Oxford University Press, 2002); Gregg Cantrell, *Stephen F. Austin: Empresario of Texas* (New Haven and London: Yale University Press, 1999), 462.

40. Thomas W. Cutrer, *Parnassus on the Mississippi: The Southern Review and the Baton Rouge Literary Community, 1935–1942* (Baton Rouge: Louisiana State University Press, 1984); Cutrer, *Ben McCulloch and the Frontier Military Tradition* (Chapel Hill: University of North Carolina Press); Robert M. Utley, *Lone Star Justice, The First Century of the Texas Rangers* (Oxford and New York: Oxford University Press, 2002); Gregg Cantrell, *Stephen F. Austin: Empresario of Texas* (New Haven and London: Yale University Press, 1999), 462.

Chapter 1

1. Family Record, n.d., Victor Marion Rose Collection, box 1 (unprocessed), Baylor University, Waco, Texas (cited hereinafter as TXC); Kathryn Stoner O'Connor, "Victor Marion Rose," in *A Republishing of the Book Most Often Known as Victor Rose's History of Victoria*, ed. J. W. Petty Jr. (Victoria: Book Mart, 1961), vii. The birth year 1842 is consistent with entries in the US censuses of 1850 in 1860, in which Victor's age is given as seven and seventeen, respectively (both used June 1 as a reference point); and he was eighteen when he enrolled in Centennial College on October 1, 1860. An incorrect birth year of 1843 was given in obituaries that appeared in the *Victoria Advocate* and the *Victoria Times* shortly after his death. The date of birth that was inscribed on a commemorative monument in Victoria's Evergreen Cemetery—January 1, 1844—is also incorrect.

2. Rose, *History of Victoria County*, 15.

3. Rose was the patriarch of a clan of frontier families whom he led to Texas, settling on claims just west of Caddo Lake. Given to booming out profanities, the big Regulator leader was nicknamed "Hell Roarin' Rose" and "The Lion of the Lake" (see "War in East Texas," *Lone Star Historian*, July 12, 2014, http://lone starhistorian2.blogspot.com/2014/07/war-in-east-texas.html). The full story of W. P. Rose will appear later in this book.

4. Roell, "Rose, Victor Marion."

5. It is interesting to note that the lives of a number of people who were to cross paths later were also at the Battle of New Orleans, such as Edward Pakenham, a relative of Nicholas Fagan, an in-law of Thomas O'Connor, James Power, empresario, and Captain Rose. There has never been any indication that they crossed paths.

6. Margaret Stoner McLean, "Rose, William Pinckney," *Handbook of Texas Online*, accessed August 17, 2014, http://www.tshaonline.org/handbook/online/articles/fro74.

7. "War in East Texas," *Lone Star Historian*, July 12, 2014, http://lonestar historian2.blogspot.com/2014/07/war-in-east-texas.html.

8. Ibid.

9. Ernest G. Fischer, *Robert Potter, Founder of the Texas Navy* (Gretna, LA: Pelican Publishing, 1976).

10. Mississippi College was the second-oldest male institution of higher learning in the state. Chartered as Hampstead Academy in 1826 and located in Mount Salus (Clinton's former name), it became Mississippi Academy in 1827. Its name was changed to Mississippi College in 1830. Charles Hillman Brough, "Historic Clinton," *Publications of the Mississippi Historical Society* 7 (1903): 285.

11. The Rose family was considered (and always considered themselves) of the higher ranks of society, making it even more interesting that Victor was able to break rank and go to work after the loss of everything his family once had.

12. Handwritten documents, n.d., 2R76314056 and 2R76314050; Kathryn Stoner O'Connor, "Memories of V. M. Rose," n.d., 2R76314049, O'Connor Family Papers, Collection of Louise S. O'Connor, Victoria, Texas. For a biographical sketch of Victor Eude Du Gaillon, see Rose, *History of Victoria County*, 124–26. For his poem "Victor Eude Du Gaillon," see Rose, *Demara*, 19.

13. He attended Rutersville College in Fayette County and Centenary College in Louisiana. (Centenary College in Jackson, Louisiana, is still an active college, and also a liberal arts college. Centenary was relocated to Shreveport, Louisiana, in 1906—it is no longer active in Jackson.) Rutersville was the first chartered Protestant College in Texas. The college flourished between 1840 and 1856. It specifically noted in a second charter in 1840, amended from the first, that it eliminated any reference to religious denomination. Later on, it went into decline due to the building of other colleges, Indian attacks, and the Mexican War.

The board of directors was engaged in land frauds with the Methodist Conference and misconduct of faculty members. It was eventually consolidated in 1856 with Texas Monumental and Military Institute. It closed in 1894 (see Judson S. Custer, "Rutersville College," *Handbook of Texas Online*, accessed December 3, 2016, http://www.tshaonline.org/handbook/online/articles/kbr17). There was also an abundance of administrative turmoil, financial instability, and external factors going on at that time. Centenary College was also a Methodist-based college in Shreveport, Louisiana, and is still in operation.

14. "John Washington Rose," Legislative Reference Library of Texas, Legislators and Leaders, http://www.lrl.state.tx.us.

15. David G. McComb, *Texas: A Modern History* (Austin: University of Texas Press, 1989), 58.

16. Further research on this is included in *No Deeper Green*, Louise O'Connor's work in progress on the Irish settlement of the Texas Coastal Bend.

17. John W. Rose to Margaret Rose, February 21, 1846 (photostat), Lawrence Sullivan Ross Letters, box 2G26, Briscoe Center for American History, University of Texas at Austin (hereafter cited as BCAH).

18. John W. Rose to Margaret Rose, February 28 and March 19, 1846, Victor Marion Rose Collection, box 1, TXC.

19. Rose, *History of Victoria County*, 186.

20. O'Connor Family Papers, Collection of Louise S. O'Connor, Victoria, Texas —2R76314058, Kathryn Stoner O'Connor, handwritten document, n.d.

21. Clow was chief clerk of the new government of Texas in 1846; by the spring of 1849, he had moved his dry goods business to nearby Port Lavaca and was soon offering cash advances on cotton. *Texas Democrat*, January 21, 1846; *Western Texan* (San Antonio), May 3, 1849; *San Antonio Ledger*, January 15, 1852.

22. Having such an emotionally detached father could have been the basis of some of Victor's later problems.

23. "Matagorda," *The Old Capitol*, July 14, 1888.

24. The Stapp and Rice families were prominent families in early US history and early Texas. See "Stapp Family History," Ancestry.com, accessed December 11, 2017, http://www.ancestry.com/name-origin?surname=stapp.

25. David G. Sansing, *The University of Mississippi: A Sesquicentennial History* (Jackson: University Press of Mississippi, 1999), 8.

26. Kathryn Stoner O'Connor, "Victor Marion Rose," introduction to Rose, *History of Victoria County*, vii.

27. "Old Subscribers of the News: Mr. J. W. Rose of Kelly, N.M., a Reader of the News for Many Years," *Galveston Daily News*, September 14, 1895.

28. O'Connor Family Papers, Collection of Louise S. O'Connor, Victoria, Texas —2R76314050, handwritten document, n.d.

29. Zilpa Rose Stoner, "Life of Zilpa Rose Stoner," August 1, 1930, Victoria County Archives, Victoria, Texas. This was yet another traumatizing experience of his youth.

30. At no period within the author's remembrance has Victoria been without good schools for the education of both genders. Among the laborers in this moral vineyard may be honorably mentioned the names of Messrs. Kilgore (about 1848); Mr. Norton (1851); Messrs. Livingston and W. R. Friend, Esq., ex-senator and learned counsel of the Cuero bar (1854); W. L. Catlender, Esq. (1859); Messrs. S. L. Kyle and Sam Wilkins (1865); Capt. Andrew P. Cunningham (1866); W. H. Allen (1859); Rev. Mr. Caldwell; Prof. Sporter; Rev. Mr. Kraph; and finally the Victoria high school, under the presidency of Prof. Wise. In 1868 St. Joseph's College was founded in Victoria through the auspices of the Catholic Church and has continued to supply a faculty of able teachers since, attended by a goodly number of students from home and abroad. In 1867 Nazareth Convent was founded, commodious houses were erected, and a number of Sisters of the Incarnate Word were introduced, principally from France, the whole being under the immediate superintendence of Madam St. Claire. Many accessions have been made to the numbers of the sisters from Victoria and contiguous counties, and the attendance of pupils is all that could be desired.

31. Victor later writes that he became friends with James Saunders Penn, of the *Laredo Times*, in Rutersville. The Penn family moved to Rutersville in 1855, so

Victor's one term at the college must have been no earlier than January of 1855. Since the college became Texas Military Institute in the summer of 1856, he had probably left by this time, as "Rutersville College" is the name used in the family records, not the newer name.

32. Rose's writings can be found on the Texas Coastal Bend Collection website: http://www.texascoastalbend.org.

33. Julia Lee Sinks, "Rutersville College," *Quarterly of the Texas State Historical Association* 2, no. 2 (1898): 127; William B. Jones, *To Survive and Excel: The Story of Southwestern University, 1840–2000* (Georgetown, TX: Southwestern University, 2006), 12.

34. John H. McLean, "Our Early Schools," *Texas Methodist Historical Quarterly* 2, no. 1 (July 1910): 64.

35. *Victoria Advocate*, April 3, 1880.

36. O'Connor, "Victor Marion Rose," viii.

37. In trying to identify who wrote letters or other information on the Stoner family, each person had one or more nicknames, often with no relationship to their given name. Because of this familial habit, some information will never be identified.

38. Kathryn Stoner O'Connor, "Memories of V. M. Rose," 2R76314049, O'Connor Family Papers, Collection of Louise S. O'Connor, Victoria, Texas.

39. Victoria County Deed Records, vol. 4, 410.

40. Julia Rose Brooking Needham, "The Brookings," submitted by Dorothy N. Whitley, *True West Magazine*, June 1976, 10–13, 48–50.

41. O'Connor Family Papers, Collection of Louise O'Connor, Victoria, Texas —2R76314049—handwritten document.

42. O'Connor, "Victor Marion Rose," vii.

43. Ibid.

44. Stoner, "Life of Zilpa Rose Stoner."

45. Sidney R. Weisiger, "Grist Mills of This Area," *Victoria Advocate*, May 10, 1970.

46. Stoner, "Life of Zilpa Rose Stoner."

47. Needham, "The Brookings," 11.

48. Stoner, "Life of Zilpa Rose Stoner."

49. For a transcription of the bill of sale, see Rose, *History of Victoria County*, 73.

50. In 1861, he was elected to the Secession Convention. In late January and early February 1861, a convention of the people of Texas met in Austin and voted to secede from the Union. Pressure to call a convention to consider secession began in October 1860, when it became apparent that Abraham Lincoln would be elected to the presidency. Walter L. Buenger, "Secession Convention," *Handbook of Texas Online*, accessed April 28, 2017, http://www.tshaonline.org/handbook/online/articles/mjs01.

51. Roy Grimes, *300 Years in Victoria County* (Victoria: Victoria Advocate Publishing, 1968), 243.

52. *Texian Advocate* (Victoria), September 23, 1854. Wheeler's lengthy de-

scription of his stock included English, French, and American prints, "latest style," muslins, "plain, figured and embroidered," tarletons, ginghams, linen and linen drilling; silk, velvet, jaconet, cottonades, flannels, lawns, dimities, and cambrics; huckaback, crash, and other towelings; quilts, counterpanes, bedspreads, curtains; collars, cuffs, chemisettes, and sleeves; buttons, ribbons, and fringe; "bleached and brown domestics," panama and leghorn hats; and bonnets "in great variety and adapted to the climate and season."

53. Nothing was known at the time about the scars of war, now diagnosed as posttraumatic stress disorder (PTSD), and alcohol was one effective means of controlling this disorder.

54. O'Connor, "Victor Marion Rose," viii.

55. Kathryn Stoner O'Connor, "Memories of V. M. Rose," n.d., 2R76314049, O'Connor Family Papers, Collection of Louise S. O'Connor, Victoria, Texas. According to the account in this document, Judge Ross sent Victor off to Centenary College on the night of the 1859 incident, but Victor did not enter Centenary until the following year. His whereabouts in that year before he entered Centenary are unknown.

56. Affidavit by F. Finger, June 25, 1860, State of Texas v. Victor M. Rose and Charles T. Wilson, No. 357, August 23, 1860, District Court, Victoria County, Victoria Regional History Center, HC-76-A, folder 13, VC/UHV Library, Victoria, Texas. "French Finger" may have been a nickname for a Frank Finger, listed in the 1860 census as a Prussian-born blacksmith in Victoria. Charles T. Wilson was a twenty-year-old printer in Victoria.

57. See State of Texas v. Victor M. Rose and Charles T. Wilson, No. 357, August 23, 1860, District Court, Victoria County, Victoria Regional History Center, HC-76-A, folder 13, VC/UHV Library, Victoria, Texas.

58. Eric J. Brock, *Centenary College of Louisiana* (Charleston, SC: Arcadia Publishing, 2000), 7–26. Jefferson Davis, future president of the Confederacy, studied both at Centenary College and at Transylvania University, where Judge Rose received his law degree.

59. Record and Matriculation Book, 1852–1907, 65, Student Records, Centenary College of Louisiana Archives and Special Collections, Shreveport, Louisiana.

60. Catalogue of the Officers and Students in Centenary College of Louisiana, 1859–60 (Baton Rouge: Daily Advocate, n.d.), 21–23.

61. Arthur M. Shaw Jr., *Centenary College Goes to War in 1861* (Shreveport: Centenary College, 1940), 5.

Chapter 2

1. Rose, *History of Victoria County*, 38.

2. J. V. Ridgely, "The Confederacy and the Martyred South," in *Nineteenth-Century Southern Literature* (Lexington: University Press of Kentucky, 1980),

77–88, accessed December 11, 2017, http://www.enotes.com/southern-litera
ture-reconstruction-criticism.

3. Rose, *History of Victoria County*, 42.

4. It has been rumored that Victor Rose did not agree with secession, but went
to war for the South anyway. His father, John Rose, voted yea for forming a convention to decide on secession. Could fear of this stigma have been the reason why
he fought for the Confederacy? "Journal of the Secession Convention of Texas,
1861," accessed December 11, 2017, https://archive.org/details/journalofsecessi
00texarich.

5. "The Texas Ordinance of Secession (February 2, 1861)," accessed December
11, 2017, http://www.lsjunction.com/docs/secesson.htm. Not everyone in Texas
was in favor of secession in 1860. Historians estimated that about 30 percent of
Texans had Unionists sentiments. These dissenters would pay a huge price for their
opinions.

6. During the Reconstruction era, those who attempted to alter the political landscape by strengthening the Republican Party in the South were labeled
"scalawags" by Southern Democrats. "Scalawags in the Civil War: Definition &
Explanation," accessed December 11, 2017, http://study.com/academy/lesson/
scalawags-in-the-civil-war-definition-lesson-quiz.html.

7. "Under the Rebel Flag: Life in Texas during the Civil War," Texas State Library
and Archives Commission, accessed December 11, 2017, https://www.tsl.texas
.gov/exhibits/civilwar/dissent.html.

8. The term "Southern Unionist" denotes those, including Texas Governor
Sam Houston, who were vocal about actively remaining with the Union. The
opponents saw secession as dangerous, illegitimate, and contrary to the inten-
tions of the founding fathers. They believed that rebelling against the United
States was dishonorable. Some even acted as spies during the war. See Maury
Klein, *Days of Defiance: Sumter, Secession, and the Coming of the Civil War* (New
York: Knopf Doubleday, 1997); Aleksandar Pavković and Peter Radan, *Creating
New States: Theory and Practice of Secession* (Farnham, UK: Ashgate Publishing,
2007), 222.

There are countless examples of those who bravely chased the very unpopular
path of resistance to the Confederacy and Secession. In one case, Tom O'Connor I,
an Irish immigrant, refused to join the Confederacy. His grandson, Thomas
O'Connor III, was to marry a Rose descendent, Kathryn Stoner O'Connor. It was
said he had to keep an army around him for protection.

9. "Voices in the Wilderness: Southerners Who Opposed Secession," South
Carolina Digital Newspaper Program, http://www.library.sc.edu.

10. "Literature of the Antebellum South—J. V. Ridgely (Essay Date 1980)."
Nineteenth-Century Literary Criticism, vol. 112, ed. Lynn M. Zott (Farmington
Hills, MI: Gale Cengage, 2002), accessed October 8, 2012, http://www.enotes
.com/literature-antebellum-south-criticism/literature-antebellum-south/j-v-ridgely
-essay-date-1980.

11. "Literature of the Antebellum South—Lewis P. Simpson (Essay Date 1973)." *Nineteenth-Century Literary Criticism*, vol. 112, ed. Lynn M. Zott (Farmington Hills, MI: Gale Cengage, 2002), accessed October 9, 2012, http://www .enotes.com/literature-antebellum-south-criticism/literature-antebellum-south/ lewis-p-simpson-essay-date-1973.

12. Victor M. Rose to Margaret Rose, May 20, 1861 (digital image), Centenary College of Louisiana Archives, Shreveport, Louisiana.

13. O'Connor, "Victor Marion Rose," ix.

14. O'Connor Family Papers, Collection of Louise O'Connor, Victoria, Texas —2R76314052—handwritten document.

15. "Drinking the Kool-Aid" is a figure of speech commonly used in the United States that refers to any person or group that knowingly goes along with a doomed or dangerous idea because of peer pressure. The phrase oftentimes carries a negative connotation when applied to an individual or group and is a reference to the 1978 cult mass suicide in Jonestown, Guyana. Jim Jones, the leader of the group, convinced his followers to move to Jonestown. Late in the year, he then ordered his flock to commit suicide by drinking grape-flavored Kool-Aid laced with potassium cyanide. In what is now commonly called "the Jonestown Massacre," 913 of the 1,100 Jonestown residents drank the Kool-Aid and died.

16. Lee Morgan, *Centenary College of Louisiana, 1825–2000: The Biography of an American Academy* (Shreveport: Centenary College of Louisiana Press, 2008), 38. The college was soon converted to a hospital for wounded Confederate soldiers. When Union forces took control of Jackson in 1863, they used campus buildings for a hospital and headquarters. The college reopened for classes in the fall of 1865.

17. Rose, *Ross' Texas Brigade*, 11.

18. Shaw, *Centenary College Goes to War in 1861*, 8.

19. One of Victor's classmates wrote a letter to his sister, Mary Pickney Rose, wanting to meet her. Letter to Mary P. Rose from L. S. Bowen, December 6, 1880, Brad Bennett Collection.

20. Victor M. Rose to Margaret Rose, October 31, 1861 (digital image), Centenary College of Louisiana Archives, Shreveport, Louisiana. Henderson "Hence" McBride Pridgen was a DeWitt County planter who served in Whitfield's Legion during the war. In his *History of Victoria County*, 39–42, Rose would include a colorful anecdote about the eccentric bachelor going off to war with elegant monogrammed blankets, worked by "fair fingers," and then courting a "buxom widow" after returning from the war.

21. John Bell Hood was a US military officer who served as a Confederate general during the Civil War (1861–65). See "John B. Hood," History.com, accessed December 11, 2017, http://www.history.com/topics/american-civil-war/ john-b-hood.

22. Rose, *Ross' Texas Brigade*, 123.

23. It is noted that Henry McCulloch is the general that called the soldiers of

the Civil War to continue to serve past the time of their enlistment. See H. E. McCulloch and T. M. Rifles, "Fellow-Soldiers of the 1st Regiment Texas Mounted Riflemen, Your Country Needs Your Services Longer," accessed December 11, 2017, https://archive.org/details/fellowsoldiersof00conf. Most thought this was going to be a war of very short duration.

24. Rose, *Ross' Texas Brigade*, 18.

25. Ibid., 19.

26. Ibid., 31.

27. Ibid., 13.

28. Rose, *History of Victoria County*, 43.

29. Ibid.

30. Ibid.

31. Ibid.

32. Abraham Lincoln brought with him certain abilities that enabled him to become an effective commander in chief. Lincoln was a fast learner and could change quickly. He withstood pressure and fatigue, yet could maintain his good judgment. He got along with people and had an extraordinary ability to cut to the heart of the matter. He could take decisive action and take responsibility. Jefferson Davis had abilities and talents, but he did not measure up to the monumental task he faced. He relied on faulty people in many cases, especially among his military leaders. He did not do well under pressure and was not good at taking decisive action. He also ignored the importance of the west. He often made wrong decisions and had bad timing. Basic insecurity harmed him. He was in poor health and of a prickly temperament, and his generals fought among themselves. His shortcomings and ill health simply prevented him from achieving all that was possible as the Confederate leader. In the end he fell short in ways that were essential to make him a great historic leader. He was a remarkable man of many talents who fell short by only the narrowest of margins. He just was not great enough. Steven E. Woodworth, *Jefferson Davis and His Generals: The Failure of the Confederate Command in the West* (Lawrence: University Press of Kansas, 1990), 305–16.

33. Rose, *Ross' Texas Brigade*, 31.

34. Ibid., 104.

35. Ibid., 84.

36. Ibid., 87.

37. Ibid.,101.

38. Ibid.,104.

39. Ibid., 114.

40. Ibid., 116.

41. Ibid.

42. Ibid., 123.

43. E. M. Coulter, *Travels in the Confederate States* (Norman: University of Oklahoma Press, 1948), 398.

44. *Bellville Countryman*, October 16, 1861.

45. Stoner, "Life of Zilpa Rose Stoner."

46. *Victoria Advocate*, February 7, 1863, reprinted in *Victoria Advocate*, June 6, 1905.

47. See Giselle Roberts, *The Confederate Belle* (Columbia: University Press of Missouri, 2003), especially "Sewing for the Soldiers," 47–50.

48. Stoner, "Life of Zilpa Rose Stoner." This could convey a lack of attention from his mother, possibly adding to his fixation on women.

49. National Archives, Compiled Service Records of Confederate Soldiers Who Served in Organizations from the State of Texas, M323, RG 109, Roll 0022.

50. Rose, *Ross' Texas Brigade*, 179–84.

51. Ibid.

52. Ibid.

53. Ibid.

54. Victor M. Rose, *The Life and Services of Gen. Ben McCulloch* (Philadelphia: Pictorial Bureau of the Press, 1888; facs. ed., Austin: Steck Company, 1858), 254.

55. Rose, *Ross' Texas Brigade*, 179–84..

56. Ibid.

57. Roell, "Rose, Victor Marion."

58. There is no "Yellow River" in Mississippi. This is most likely the Yazoo River. The only Yellow River is a tributary off the Mississippi in Iowa.

59. Author's note: This belied the constant comments about the "loving darkies" and their loyalty to their masters. There were some instances of this, but certainly not all stayed with the owner's families.

60. Rose, *History of Victoria County*, xii.

61. Rose, *Ross' Texas Brigade*, 8.

Chapter 3

1. O'Connor Family Papers, Collection of Louise S. O'Connor, Victoria, Texas.

2. Margaret Stoner McLean interview with Louise S. O'Connor, Georgetown, Texas, July 24, 1997.

3. Cash, *The Mind of the South*, 75–80.

4. "Oral Memoirs of Mary Margaret Stoner McLean," by Lois E. Myers, Family Life & Community History Project—Baylor University Institute for Oral History, 31.

5. Rose, *History of Victoria County*, 58.

6. Grimes, *300 Years in Victoria County*, 329.

7. Cash, *The Mind of the South*, 112–18. The Ku Klux Klan is a secret organization of white Southerners formed after the US Civil War to fight black emancipation and Northern domination.

8. Rose, *History of Victoria County*, xiii.

9. A writ issued by a court to the sheriff of a county to bring in a defendant having failed to appear in court.

10. "Dismissed" is written on a worn envelope with the notations "370" and "The State of Texas vs. Victor Rose." See State of Texas v. Victor M. Rose, No. 370, District Court, Victoria County, Victoria Regional History Center, HC-76-A, folders 34 and 40, VC/UHV Library, Victoria, Texas.

11. Cash, *The Mind of the South*, 92.

12. Stoner, "Life of Zilpa Rose Stoner."

13. Rose, *History of Victoria County*, 186; Victor M. Rose to John Henry Brown, December 25, 1883, John Henry Brown Family Papers, box 2E58, BCAH. A poem was written by Father Ryan entitled "The Conquered Banner." It is reminiscent of Victor's writing style.

14. Rose, *History of Victoria County*, 54. To "plead the baby act," a slang phrase, is to make excuses by pretending ignorance or inexperience. Lincoln had used the phrase when addressing the jury in an 1841 court case.

15. Abigail Curlee, "A Study of Texas Slave Plantations, 1822–1865," PhD diss., University of Texas, 1932, 299, 300.

16. Rose, *History of Victoria County*, 63.

17. Stoner, "Life of Zilpa Rose Stoner."

18. Victoria County Deed Records, vol. 10, 16–17.

19. Kathryn Stoner O'Connor Notes, n.d., Collection of Louise S. O'Connor, Victoria, Texas.

20. O'Connor, "Victor Marion Rose," viii.

21. Ibid., xiii.

22. Stoner, "Life of Zilpa Rose Stoner."

23. "Random Shots," Victor Marion Rose Collection, box 1, TXC. The original handwritten poem has just been found in the Matt Williamson Collection, donated to Louise O'Connor by Brad Bennett, 2017.

24. Phyllis A. McKenzie, "Margaret Heffernan Borland," in *Texas Women on the Cattle Trails*, ed. Sara R. Massey (College Station: Texas A&M University Press, 2006), 100.

25. Rose, *History of Victoria County*, 131.

26. Needham, "The Brookings," 10–13, 40–50.

27. Ibid.

28. In the same epidemic, Victor's mother-in-law, Mrs. Borland, lost four children and a grandson. O'Connor, "Victor Marion Rose," xii.

29. Margaret McLean, "Tournaments: An Account of This Early Sport in Victoria, Texas and Neighboring Communities," *The Cattleman*, September 1, 1948.

30. Ibid. *Waverley* is a historical novel by Sir Walter Scott (1771–1832). Published anonymously in 1814 as Scott's first venture into prose fiction, it is often regarded as the first historical novel in the Western tradition. The book became so popular that Scott's later novels were advertised as being "by the author of *Waverley*." His series of works on similar themes written during the same period have become collectively known as the "Waverley novels."

31. O'Connor, "Victor Marion Rose," vii.

32. *Victoria Advocate*, February 26, 1870.

33. Ibid.

34. Ibid. Gilbert, a former member of the 6th Texas Infantry, wrote columns during the war for the *Houston Telegraph* under the name "High Private." See Mary M. Cronin, "R. R. Gilbert: A Texas Humorist Goes to War," in *Knights of the Quill: Confederate Correspondents and Their Civil War Reporting*, ed. Patricia G. McNeely et al. (West Lafayette, IN: Purdue University Press, 2010), 465–82. Marcus Mills "Brick" Pomeroy was a controversial journalist who wrote a column titled "Our Saturday Night" for his La Crosse, Wisconsin, newspaper; a Union loyalist, he frequently denounced Lincoln and his policies.

35. *Lavaca Commercial*, reprinted in *Galveston Daily News*, July 23, 1870; see also *Evening Telegraph* (Houston), July 14, 1870.

Chapter 4

1. H. L. Bentley and Thomas Pilgrim, *The Texas Legal Directory for 1876–77* (Austin: Democratic Statesman Office, 1877), 60.

2. Leopold Morris, *Pictorial History of Victoria and Victoria County* (San Antonio: Clemons Printing Co., 1953).

3. Thomas R. Cocke to Victor M. Rose, May 4, 1872, Victor Marion Rose Papers, 1832–87, box 2G28, BCAH.

4. Victoria County Deed Records, vol. 11, pp. 482–83; vol. 13, pp. 307–8, 336–37. The estate of John W. Rose was officially declared settled, and Margaret Rose's duties as executrix fully discharged in September of 1870. See Victoria County Probate Minutes, vol. A-3, 248.

5. Victoria County Probate Minutes, vol. A-3, 244, 347, 383.

6. Margaret Borland, a Victoria rancher, was born in Ireland in 1824 and was one of the Irish colonists who arrived in Texas with the McMullen-McGloin colony. She was said to be the only woman known to have led a cattle drive. James C. McNutt, "Borland, Margaret Heffernan," *Handbook of Texas Online*, accessed December 11, 2017, http://www.tshaonline.org/handbook/online/articles/fbo72.

7. Receipt signed by James Heffernan, Margaret Borland Papers, box 3H74, BCAH.

8. Margaret Borland estate, Victoria County Probate Minutes, vol. 4, p. 118, cited by Phyllis A. McKenzie, "Margaret Heffernan Borland," *Texas Women on the Cattle Trails*, ed. Sara R. Massey (College Station: Texas A&M University Press, 2006), 107, 117n139. According to the *Wichita Eagle* of July 31, 1873, Thomas Sterne Jr., a Victoria cattleman, made the trip to Kansas to settle Borland's affairs relating to her livestock.

9. Needham, "The Brookings," 11.

10. *Galveston Daily News*, October 15, 1974.

11. Needham, "The Brookings," 11; Historical Marker Application, Brooking-Lipscomb-White Home, March 26, 1987, Texas Historical Commission, Austin, Texas, Portal to Texas History, http://texashistory.unt.edu/ark:/67531/metapth477895/.

12. Interview with Mary Margaret Stoner McLean by Lois E. Myers, Oral History Memoir, Baylor University Institute for Oral History, April 29, 1987, 14.

13. In April 1876, Edwin Upshur (also Upshire) Brooking was confronted by a group of vigilantes informing him that they "could not tolerate him in the community any longer" and that they would give him three days to leave Goliad County. *Galveston Daily News*, April 7, 1876. A few months later, Ady (Adolph) Milde "of the Brooking party" was forcibly removed from Goliad. *Victoria Advocate*, August 24, 1876. Another brother, Robert Brooking, was charged with cattle rustling, but the case was dismissed in 1885 for insufficient evidence. *Victoria Weekly Advocate*, November 21, 1885; cited in *Victoria Daily Advocate*, November 13, 1915.

14. Interview with Margaret Stoner McLean by Louise O'Connor, August 29, 1997.

15. Having Native American blood in the family would have also been a stumbling block for the Brookings.

16. Interview with Margaret Stoner McLean by Louise O'Connor, August 29, 1997.

17. Clara Nickelson Brooking was the niece of Milton Hardy, Julia Hardy Rose's father. Her father, J. L. Nickelson, ran a hotel in Victoria (Rose, *History of Victoria County*, 138). She was the second wife of Edwin Upshur Brooking. His daughter from his first marriage, Emma Brooking, married Victor's youngest brother, Preston Rose.

18. Deposition of Martha J. Wigginton, September 19, 1878, Victoria County, 3.

19. Petition of Ada A. Rose, March 2, 1878, Williamson County District Court, Case No. 1745, Ada Brooking Rose v. Victor Marion Rose, 1–2.

20. Ibid., 3.

21. Ibid., 3–4.

22. Deposition of Clara Brooking, September 11, 1878, Victoria County, pp. 1–2. Deposition of Martha J. Wigginton, September 19, 1878, Victoria County, pp. 2, 4. Deposition of J. L. Nickelson, September 1, 1878, Victoria County, 2.

23. Case no. 1745, September 1878, Williamson County, Texas, District Court.

24. Note that the age difference between Victor and Ada also could have posed an additional problem in an already troubled marriage.

25. Victoria County Deed Records, vol. 16, 557–58; Rose, *History of Victoria County*, 186. Margaret Rose and her two sons would continue to move around, perhaps in a search of better land. In 1887 Adam Summers petitioned Governor Ross for aid, recounting his suffering as a result of drought conditions (*Galveston Daily News*, January 26, 1887).

26. Stoner, "Life of Zilpa Rose Stoner."

27. "Oral Memoirs of Mary Margaret Stoner McLean," 56.

28. Victoria County Probate Minutes, vol. 3A, 525, 532, 536, 729, 730, 747.

29. *Victoria Advocate*, August 30, 1879.

30. *Victoria Advocate*, September 13, 1879.

31. *Austin Weekly Statesman*, August 15, 1878.

32. See, for example, letters in the Victor Marion Rose Papers, 1832–87, box 2G28, BCAH.

33. *Victoria Advocate*, June 15, 1878.

34. The Despenadores fraternity existed in Castile toward the close of the fourteenth century. It had for its principal object the dispatching of the sick, after the last rites of the church had been performed, "to make sure that the soul should realize the object of absolution and not be subjected to the temptations of sin again by assuming its place in the walks of life."

35. Victor M. Rose, *Los Despenadores—A Spanish Story* (Austin: State Book & Job Office, 1878), 4.

36. Handwritten documents, n.d., 2R76314056; Kathryn Stoner O'Connor, "Memories of V. M. Rose," O'Connor Family Papers, Collection of Louise S. O'Connor, Victoria, Texas.

37. Ibid.

Chapter 5

1. *The Texas Vendetta; Or, The Sutton-Taylor Feud, Ross' Texas Brigade, Demara, the Comanche Queen, Some Historical Facts in Regard to the Settlement of Victoria, Texas: Its Progress and Present Status, Celeste Valcœur, While the Spell of Her Witchery Lingers,* and *The Life and Services of Gen. Ben McCulloch.*

2. O'Connor Family Papers, Collection of Louise S. O'Connor, Victoria, Texas, 2R76314050—handwritten document.

3. Ibid.

4. *Victoria Advocate*, August 7, 1880.

5. Galls are abnormal growths that occur on leaves, twigs, or branches (see http://www.missouribotanicalgarden.org). Manada is a breeding band of wild horses (see https://www.merriam-webster.com/dictionary/manada).

6. These two rivers join close to the Texas coast.

7. "Kemper Kernals," *Victoria Advocate*, August 7, 1880 The Stuarts are not extinct. Their home is Mount Stuart, on the Isle of Bute.

8. *Victoria Advocate*, May 29, 1880.

9. "Thrall's History of Texas," *Victoria Advocate*, April 3, 1880.

10. "Kemper Kernals," *Victoria Advocate*, October 9, 1880. Thrall's detractors were legion, and one of the harshest reviews of the book was written by Temple Houston, the youngest child of Sam Houston. "Its title to 'history' is fatally defective, because of its glaring inaccuracies and numerous errors," wrote Houston; see "A Review of Thrall's History of Texas," *Galveston Daily News*, September 26, 1880. Rose refers to this review in his October 9 column.

11. "Wishes to Correct: More Facts in Early Texan History—The Story of Indian Cannabalism Repeated, But Somewhat Moderated—Investigation Reveals the Truth," *Victoria Advocate*, April 24, 1880.

12. "The Correction Accepted," *Victoria Advocate*, May 1, 1880.

13. Charles August Leuschner was from Prussia. His family settled in Victoria, where his father worked as a carpenter. He fought in the Civil War. Returning to Victoria, he worked as a trail driver, a barber, a city band member; was a city alderman; and was active in politics. Victor Rose considered him a friend and a war hero. "Charles August Leuschner," Victoria Regional History Center, accessed December 11, 2017, http://vrhc.uhv.edu/manuscripts/leuschner.aspx.

14. "Incidents of the Past: Events Connected with the Army of Tennessee during the Late War," *Victoria Advocate*, December 11, 1880. The remaining parts of Leuschner's diary appeared on December 18 and 25.

15. "The Farming Interests of Victoria County," *Victoria Advocate*, April 24, 1880. It should be noted that there was a prejudice against "sod busting" among ranchers. It was considered a desecration of the land.

16. Another exception is Reuben Potter's articles on the Texas Revolution, which appeared in eastern magazines and newspapers in the 1870s and 1880s. According to one historiographer, "Potter confined his historical writing to a series of articles on specific topics rather than attempting a comprehensive history or a single volume." Laura Lyons McLemore, *Inventing Texas: Early Historians of the Lone Star State* (College Station: Texas A&M University Press, 2004), 77.

17. If a sword of Damocles hangs over someone, they are in a situation where something bad is likely to happen to them at any moment. This phrase comes from a story about Damocles, who had to eat his food with a sword hanging over him that was tied up by a single hair.

18. Victor M. Rose, *The Texas Vendetta; or, The Sutton-Taylor Feud* (New York: J. J. Little & Company, 1880), 3.

19. Rose, *The Texas Vendetta*, 11.

20. Ibid.

21. Kathy Weiser, "Texas Legends: The Sutton-Taylor Feud of DeWitt County," Legends of America, accessed December 11, 2017, http://www.legends ofamerica.com/tx-suttontaylor.html; Rose, *The Texas Vendetta*.

22. Rose, *The Texas Vendetta*, 69.

23. Rose, *Ross' Texas Brigade*, 6, 7.

24. It should be noted that many of the volunteer soldiers in the Texas Revolution were teenagers.

25. Rose, *Ross' Texas Brigade*, 15, 21.

26. Ibid, 114.

27. E. M. Coulter, *Travels in the Confederate States*, 398.

28. Rose's influence can be seen in works by authors such as Gregg Cantrell and Thomas W. Cutrer.

29. Rose, *Demara*, 3.

30. In a speech delivered at Seguin on July 12, 1873, Ireland explained his opposition to the railroad monopolies, which earned him the nickname "Ox-Cart John." For the full text, see "Speech of Hon. John Ireland," *Weekly Democratic Statesman* (Austin), July 31, 1873.

31. Translation—It is sweet to play the fool.

32. Translation—Long live trifles.

33. Rose, *Demara*, 76.

34. Translation—Lost.

35. Rose, *Demara*, 32.

36. George W. Paschal (1841–1917) was the son of George Washington Paschal and Sarah Ridge Paschal and lived in Galveston in the late 1840s and early 1850s. The two boys perhaps became friends when Victor and his family were living at Saluria. Both boys' fathers were lawyers. But unlike John Rose, George Washington Paschal was a strong Union supporter. He became a distinguished legal scholar and authored, among other works, *A Digest of the Laws of Texas* (1866). Amelia W. Williams, "Paschal, George Washington," *Handbook of Texas Online*, accessed December 11, 2017, http://www.tshaonline.org/handbook/on line/articles/fpa46.

37. We should note that the Comanche were paid by Mexico to continue depredations against Texas.

38. Timothy Egan, *Short Nights of the Shadow Catcher: The Epic Life and Immortal Photographs of Edward Curtis* (New York: Houghton Mifflin Harcourt, 2012), 6.

39. There is a plan afoot to once again publish this book.

40. Victor M. Rose to John Henry Brown, August 11, 1889, cited in John H. Jenkins, *Texas Basic Books: An Annotated Bibliography of Selected Works for a Research Library*, rev. ed. (Austin: Texas State Historical Association, 1988), 346.

41. Rose, *History of Victoria County*, 66–73.

42. Ibid., 32.

43. Ibid., 89.

44. Ibid., 92.

45. Ibid., 211.

46. *Galveston Daily News*, January 14, 1886.

47. John A. Adams Jr., *Conflict and Commerce on the Rio Grande: Laredo, 1755–1955* (College Station: Texas A&M University Press, 2008), 102, 103; Violet Cearley, "Penn, James Saunders," *Handbook of Texas Online*, accessed December 11, 2017, http://www.tshaonline.org/handbook/online/articles/fpekn.

48. *Myrtle Springs Herald*, July 8, 1891, reprinted in *Laredo Times*, July 12, 1891.

49. "Dear Old Charley." *The Laredo Times*, July 25, 1884.

50. "Col. Victor M. Rose" is described as "a writer of no mean reputation" in John H. McLean, "Our Early Schools," 64. A niece wrote, "Uncle Vic usually went by the name of Colonel V. M. Rose." Needham, "The Brookings," 11.

51. *Galveston Daily News*, May 10, 1887.

52. *Floresville Chronicle*, reprinted in *Galveston Daily News*, July 27, 1886.

53. *Gulf News* (Corpus Christi), reprinted in *Brenham Weekly Banner*, February 5, 1891.

54. *Galveston Daily News*, July 3, 1887.

55. Letter from Victor Rose to John Henry Brown, October 20, 1889, TXC.

56. Letter from Victor Rose to John Henry Brown, January 25, 1886, TXC.

57. Ibid.

58. Rose, *The Life and Services of Gen. Ben McCulloch*, 150. McCulloch hesitated on the attack because his unit was seriously depleted. It had started to rain, and he didn't want to ruin the little ammunition they had. By hesitating on his march, the enemy advanced. He basically had no other choice than to give it their all with what little they had. They were victorious.

59. Letter from Victor Rose to John Henry Brown, July 15, 1887, TXC.

60. Letter from Victor Rose to John Henry Brown, February 17, 1887, TXC.

61. Letter from Victor Rose to John Henry Brown, August 22, 1888, TXC.

62. *The Old Capitol*, reprinted in *Galveston Daily News*, March 7, 1889.

63. *Galveston Daily News*, May 9, 1886.

64. "Bound with a hundred brazen knots behind his back, he roars horribly with blood-stained mouth."

65. M. R. Perron to Manager, Victoria Chamber of Commerce, February 12, 1957, Sidney Roper Weisinger Collection, W9-152, Victoria Regional History Center, Victoria, Texas; see also "Mr. Jessel" in Rose, *History of Victoria County*, 140.

66. O'Connor, "Victor Marion Rose," xiii. In 1891 Melita Perron married one of Laredo's customs inspectors; see *Laredo Weekly Times*, May 16, 1915.

67. Unlike the primary where residents simply cast their ballots, a caucus is a local gathering where voters openly decide which candidate to support. A small band of devoted volunteers all exert an outsized influence in the open setting of a caucus. This allows a delegate or candidate with the most votes in a state's primary or caucus to win the right to represent all of the party's delegates at the National Convention.

68. Victor M. Rose, *While the Spell of Her Witchery Lingers, and Other Poems* (Laredo, TX: n.p., 1886), 17–18.

69. Victor M. Rose, *The Life and Services of Gen. Ben McCulloch*, 121.

70. Letter from Victor M. Rose to John Henry Brown, December 14, 1883, Victor Marion Rose Collection, TXC.

71. Letter from Jefferson Davis to Victor M. Rose, October 23, 1883, Lawrence Sullivan Ross Letters, box 2G26, BCAH.

72. Again we see people relevant to the story, later timely connections, and so on, all meeting or being at significant places or events in history. Author's Note: Fagan, Pakenham, TOC, McCullough, Rose—Do we need to establish a connection with these people? Having been at San Jacinto, a relative-to-be in later years named Tom O'Connor may have seen him and vice versa, as O'Connor was in the Battle of San Jacinto. This relationship will be followed in a coming book, *No Deeper Green*, about the Irish settlement of the Texas Coastal Bend.

73. Letter from Henry E. McCulloch to John Henry Brown, December 8, 1883, John Henry Brown Papers, box 2E58, folder 10, BCAH.

74. Letter from John Henry Brown to Henry E. McCulloch, June 4, 1884, John Henry Brown Papers, box 2E58, BCAH.

75. Letter from Victor M. Rose to John Henry Brown, August 1887, Victor Marion Rose Collection, box 2B214, folder 1, TXC.

76. *Galveston Daily News*, August 3, 1889.

77. Victor M. Rose, "A Peep into History," *The Victoria Advocate* (Victoria), December 4, 1880, vol. XXXIV, no. 34. Lately there has been a redress of thought about Alexander Hamilton and his unequaled brilliance that so rings true today in ways that were almost prophetic for the time.

Chapter 6

1. O'Connor Family Papers, Collection of Louise S. O'Connor, Victoria, Texas —2R76314056, handwritten document, n.d.

2. In September 1836, Columbia, now known as West Columbia, became capital of the Republic of Texas. In April 1837, at the wish of President Houston, the seat of government was moved to more adequate quarters in the city of Houston. "West Columbia, Texas," TexasEscapes.com, accessed December 11, 2017, http://texasescapes.com/TexasGulfCoastTowns/West-Columbia-Texas.htm.

3. Mordello Stephen Munson Papers, Center for American History, box 3K440, folder 3.

4. Mordello Munson and *The Old Capitol* Formation, Mordello Stephen Munson Papers, Briscoe Center for American History, University of Texas, Austin, Texas, Box 3K440, Folder 3.

5. *Edna Progress*, reprinted in *Galveston Daily News*, September 16, 1888.

6. Wilma Ratchford Craig, *Ratchfords . . . I Reckon* (Baltimore: Gateway Press, 1971), 367–68.

7. See, for example, *Galveston Daily News*, July 3, 1904; *Weekly Advocate* (Victoria), January 26, 1907.

8. His *Life and Services of Gen. Ben McCulloch* is cited as a primary source into the twenty-first century.

9. "Literature of the Antebellum South—R. S. Cotterill (Essay Date 1939)," *Nineteenth-Century Literary Criticism*, vol. 112, ed. Lynn M. Zott (Farmington Hills, MI: Gale Cengage, 2002), accessed September 16, 2012, http://www.enotes.com/literature-antebellum-south-criticism/literature-antebellum-south/r-s-cotterill-essay-date-1939.

10. In 1889, September 11, G. W. Fulton writes to an unknown recipient that he cannot fund Victor's book due to low funds, also noting that he may be a genius but is imprudent about money matters.

11. Victor M. Rose to M. S. Munson, November 12, 1887, Munson Family Papers, box 3K440, folder 3, BCAH. In rejecting Brazoria because of its political climate, Rose is probably referring to tensions between two white organizations, the Tax Payers Association, of which Munson was the president, and the Law and Order Association. Both were formed to combat the influence of Union Leagues, agencies of the Republican Party that attempted to control the black vote. See

James A. Creighton, *A Narrative History of Brazoria County* (Waco: Texian Press, 1975), 268–69. The two organizations merged in March 1888 (*The Old Capitol*, March 10 and 17, 1888). At the time Rose arrived in Brazoria County, there was also racial unrest. The murder of a black constable who was attempting to serve a writ on a white man had resulted in episodes of violence throughout Brazoria and Matagorda counties. See "From the Seat of War: Some Facts about the Uprising," *Galveston Daily News*, September 28, 1887.

12. *The Old Capitol*, December 24, 1887.

13. *The Old Capitol*. March 3, 1888.

14. *The Old Capitol*, January 7, 1888.

15. His somewhat unique sense of humor could still be found in the Rose-Stoner descendants.

16. *The Old Capitol*, February 18, 1888.

17. *The Old Capitol*, February 25, 1888.

18. *The Old Capitol*, February 24, 1888.

19. Ibid.

20. Ibid.

21. It can be noted that many words he used are still in the language of his descendants. His flowery, classically related terms were passed down to following generations.

22. *The Old Capitol*, April 14, 1888.

23. If you have ever tasted a good dewberry, you can understand his enthusiasm about them.

24. *The Old Capitol*, May 26, 1888.

25. William Henry Crain, Texas senator and United States congressman, was born in 1848. He was elected district attorney for the Twenty-Third Judicial District in 1872, and was elected to the Texas Senate as a Democrat in 1876. He canvassed the state for the Democratic Party during several presidential elections, and served as a member of the national Democratic convention in 1880. Crain was elected as a Democrat from the Seventh District to the Forty-Ninth United States Congress. He served in the five succeeding congresses, where he opposed prohibition and, unlike most Texas Democratic congressmen, opposed the free coinage of silver in the 1890s, supporting President Grover Cleveland's fiscal policies. He was known as a "beautiful and fluent speaker." See Craig H. Roell, "Crain, William Henry," *Handbook of Texas Online*, accessed May 10, 2017, http://www.tshaonline.org/handbook/online/articles/fcr01.

26. *The Old Capitol*, September 8, 1888.

27. *The Old Capitol*, July 28, 1888.

28. Hobart Huson, *Refugio: A Comprehensive History of Refugio County from Aboriginal Times to 1955*, vol. II (Woodsboro, TX: The Rooke Foundation, 1955), 165.

29. *The Old Capitol*, August 3, 1889.

30. Letter from Victor Rose to John Henry Brown, *The Old Capitol*, August 5, 1889, TXC.

31. Charles Henderson Yoakum (1849–1909)—attorney, state legislator, and US Congressman. Born near Tehuacana, Texas, attorney and friend of Sam Houston, and author of a two-volume history of Texas published in 1855. Brian Hart, "Yoakum, Charles Henderson," *Handbook of Texas Online*, accessed May 2, 2017, http://www.tshaonline.org/handbook/online/articles/fyo02.

32. *The Old Capitol*, September 8, 1888.

33. *The Old Capitol*, September 29, 1888.

34. Norris Wright Cuney (1846–98)—politician, born to a white planter and a slave mother near Hempstead, Texas. Served as a delegate to every national Republican convention from 1872 to 1892, was alderman on Galveston City Council in 1883, and first grand master of the Prince Hall Masons in Texas from 1875 to 1877. Rob Fink, "Turner, Clyde Douglas [Bulldog]," *Handbook of Texas Online*, accessed May 2, 2017, http://www.tshaonline.org/handbook/online/articles/ftu25.

35. *The Old Capitol*, May 28, 1889.

36. There are three other editions of the paper on file at the Briscoe Center for American History, dated 6/5/1889, Vol II No XXVII, 6/29/1889 Vol II No [XXIX?], 7/20/1889 Vol II No XXXII.

Chapter 7

1. Letter from Victor M. Rose to Henry E. McCulloch, September 22, 1889 (copy), John Henry Brown Papers, box 2E58, folder 10, BCAH. In copying Rose's original letter, McCulloch may have misinterpreted "W. C." as "W. T."

2. In his *History of Victoria County*, Rose called William Cole Terry (1834–1908) "a gentleman of profuse liberality and hospitality; a big-hearted, generous friend" (p. 200). In 1882 Terry was a candidate for Victoria County sheriff (*Victoria Advocate*, September 30, 1882); by 1900 he was a land and stock agent for the San Antonio and Arkansas Passenger Railway (*Houston Daily Post*, July 29, 1900). W. C. Terry was the elder brother of Pickett ("Pick") Hercules Terry (1837–1904), who edited the *Rockport Transcript*. He was evidently known as "The Bard of Arkansas" (see *History of Victoria County*, 200).

3. In 1961, when Kathryn O'Connor's biographical sketch of Rose was published in the reprinted edition of *History of Victoria County*, she noted that "a manuscript of the life of Henry McCulloch remains unpublished" (Rose, *History of Victoria County*, xiv). After Dr. Pat Ireland Nixon, a past president of the Texas State Historical Association, wrote to O'Connor to inquire about the manuscript, he shared her reply in the organization's periodical: "As to your inquiry about the manuscripts of the Henry McCulloch history, I am sorry to have to admit that only a few pages of it exist. As a child I remember my mother, Victor M. Rose's sister, let us cut up for paper dolls pages and pages of the stacks of paper on which I remember spelling out the name of Henry McCulloch. I have only the few pages left" (*Southwestern Historical Quarterly* 66 [July 1962]: 172). The discrepancy is

puzzling. I actually saw what appeared to be a full manuscript on Henry McCulloch in the 1970s at St. Dennis Church, Refugio County, Texas.

4. Victor M. Rose, *Stephen F. Austin, In the Balances* (n.p., 1890).

5. Letter from Victor Rose to John Henry Brown, July 4, 1889, TXC.

6. Sterling C. Robertson and Jose Maria Balmaceda, "[Texas Colonial Manuscript] English Translation of the 1831 Stephen F. Austin and Samuel M. Williams Grant (Austin Colony), made for Sterling C. Robertson in 1833," accessed August 19, 2013, http://www.raremaps.com.

7. Letter from Victor M. Rose to G. W. Fulton, September 6, 1889, John Henry Brown Papers, box 2E54, folder 2, BCAH.

8. Gregg Cantrell, *Stephen F. Austin Empresario of Texas* (New Haven and London: Yale University Press, 1999).

9. Rose, *Stephen F. Austin, In the Balances*, 5.

10. Letter from Victor M. Rose to John Henry Brown, May 10, 1890, Victor Marion Rose Collection, box 2B214, folder 3, TXC.

11. *Waxahachie Enterprise*, reprinted in *Galveston Daily News*, March 24, 1875. See also *Galveston Daily News*, May 13, 1875.

12. Letter from W. P. Zuber to Guy M. Bryan, December 1, 1890, William Physick Zuber Papers, box 2H427, BCAH.

13. See "Points about Politics: The Official Returns of the Late Election," *Galveston Daily News*, November 13, 1890.

14. Letter from Victor M. Rose to John Henry Brown, August 5, 1889, Victor Marion Rose Collection, box 2B214, folder 3, TXC.

15. A loud character in the Robert Burns poem, "Tam O'Shanter, who brought disaster upon himself by his braying."

16. "The State Press. What the Papers throughout Texas Are Talking About." *Dallas Morning News*, February 29, 1892.

17. *Myrtle Springs Herald*, August 27, 1891.

18. Family Record, n.d., Victor Marion Rose Collection, box 1, TXC.

19. *Galveston Daily News*, September 14, 1895.

20. Victor M. Rose to John Henry Brown, July 12, 1889, Victor Marion Rose Collection, 2B214, folder 3, TXC.

21. *Victoria Advocate*, October 31, 1891.

22. *Victoria Times*, reprinted in *Galveston Daily News*, January 30, 1893. The *Brenham Daily Banner* of January 29, 1893, also reported a death date of January 21 and described Rose as "an old Texas editor and historian."

23. Kathryn Stoner O'Connor, "Victor Marion Rose," in *History of Victoria County: A Republishing of the Book Most Often Known as Victor Rose's History of Victoria*, ed. J. W. Petty Jr. (Victoria: Book Mart, 1961), xiii; Stoner, "Life of Zilpa Rose Stoner."

24. *Victoria Advocate*, reprinted in *Galveston Daily News*, February 1, 1893.

25. *Weekly Advocate* (Victoria), January 26, 1907.

Epilogue

1. Rose, *History of Victoria County*, 92–94.

Appendix 3

1. Sam H. Dixon, *The Poets and Poetry of Texas* (Austin: Sam H. Dixon & Co., 1885), 268–70.

BIBLIOGRAPHY

Archives of Papers Related to Victor Marion Rose and His Family

Adina de Zavala Collection, Special Collections, University of Texas at Arlington Libraries.

John Henry Brown Papers, Briscoe Center for American History, University of Texas at Austin, Texas.

Lawrence Sullivan Ross Letters, Briscoe Center for American History, University of Texas at Austin.

Mordello Stephen Munson Papers, Briscoe Center for American History, University of Texas at Austin.

O'Connor Family Papers, Collection of Louise S. O'Connor, Victoria, Texas.

Victor Marion Rose Collection, Texas Collection, Baylor University, Waco, Texas

Victor Marion Rose Papers, 1832–1887, Briscoe Center for American History, University of Texas at Austin.

Victoria Regional History Center, VC/UHV Library, Victoria, Texas.

William Physick Zuber Papers, Briscoe Center for American History, University of Texas at Austin.

Publications

Adams Jr., John A. *Conflict and Commerce on the Rio Grande: Laredo, 1755–1955.* College Station: Texas A&M University Press, 2008.

Austin Weekly Statesman, Austin, Texas.

Bellville Countryman, Bellville, Texas.

Bentley, H. L., and Thomas Pilgrim. *The Texas Legal Directory for 1876–77.* Austin: Democratic Statesman Office, 1877.

Brenham Weekly Banner, Brenham, Texas.

Brock, Eric J. *Centenary College of Louisiana.* Charleston, SC: Arcadia Publishing, 2000.

Brough, Charles Hillman. "Historic Clinton." *Publications of the Mississippi Historical Society* 7 (1903).

Buenger, Walter L. "Secession Convention." *Handbook of Texas Online*, April 28, 2017, http://www.tshaonline.org/handbook/online/articles/mjs01.

Cantrell, Gregg. *Stephen F. Austin: Empresario of Texas*. New Haven: Yale University Press, 1999.

Cash, W. J. *The Mind of the South*. New York: Vintage Books, 1991.

Catalogue of the Officers and Students in Centenary College of Louisiana, 1859–60. Baton Rouge: Daily Advocate, n.d.

"Compiled Service Records of Confederate Soldiers Who Served in Organizations from the State of Texas." National Archives.

Coulter, E. M. *Travels in the Confederate States*. Norman: University of Oklahoma Press, 1948.

Craig, Wilma Ratchford. *Ratchfords . . . I Reckon*. Baltimore: Gateway Press, 1971.

Cronin, Mary M. "R.R. Gilbert: A Texas Humorist Goes to War." In *Knights of the Quill: Confederate Correspondents and Their Civil War Reporting*, edited by Patricia G. McNeely et al. West Lafayette, IN: Purdue University Press, 2010.

Curlee, Abigail. "A Study of Texas Slave Plantations, 1822–1865." PhD diss., University of Texas, 1932.

Custer, Judson S. "Rutersville College." *Handbook of Texas Online*, September 15, 2012, http://www.tshaonline.org/handbook/online/articles/kbr17.

Cutrer, Thomas W. *Ben McCulloch and the Frontier Military Tradition*. Chapel Hill: University of North Carolina Press, 1993.

———. *Parnassus on the Mississippi: The Southern Review and the Baton Rouge Literary Community, 1935–1942*. Baton Rouge: Louisiana State University Press, 1984.

Dallas Morning News, Dallas, Texas.

Degler, Carl N. "The Foundation of Southern Distinctiveness." *The Southern Review* 13, no. 2 (April 1977).

de la Teja, Jesus. *Lone Star Unionism, Dissent, and Resistance: Other Sides of Civil War Texas*. Norman: University of Oklahoma Press, 2016.

Dixon, Sam H. *The Poets and Poetry of Texas*. Austin: Sam H. Dixon & Co., 1885.

Egan, Timothy. *Short Nights of the Shadow Catcher: The Epic Life and Immortal Photographs of Edward Curtis*. New York: Houghton Mifflin Harcourt, 2012.

Evening Telegraph, Houston, Texas.

Fink, Rob. "Turner, Clyde Douglas [Bulldog]." *Handbook of Texas Online*, May 2, 2017, http://www.tshaonline.org/handbook/online/articles/ftu25.

Fischer, Ernest G. *Robert Potter, Founder of the Texas Navy*. Gretna, LA: Pelican Publishing, 1976.

Floresville Chronicle, Floresville, Texas.

Galveston Daily News, Galveston, Texas.

Grimes, Roy. *300 Years in Victoria County*. Victoria, TX: Victoria Advocate Publishing, 1968.

Gulf News, Corpus Christi, Texas.

Hart, Brian. "Yoakum, Charles Henderson." *Handbook of Texas Online*, May 2, 2017, http://www.tshaonline.org/handbook/online/articles/fy002.

Hunter, Hon. Robert Mercer Taliaferro. "Origin of the Late War." *Southern Historical Society Papers*, I, January (1876), August 19, 2013, http://www.civilwar home.com/warorigin.htm.

Huson, Hobart. *Refugio: A Comprehensive History of Refugio County from Aboriginal Times to 1955,*vol. II. Woodsboro, TX: The Rooke Foundation, 1955.

Isenberg, Nancy. *White Trash: The 400-Year Untold History of Class in America.* New York: Viking, 2016.

Jenkins, John H. *Texas Basic Books: An Annotated Bibliography of Selected Works for a Research Library,* rev. ed. Austin: Texas State Historical Association, 1988.

Jones, William B. *To Survive and Excel: The Story of Southwestern University, 1840–2000.* Georgetown, TX: Southwestern University, 2006.

Klein, Maury. *Days of Defiance: Sumter, Secession, and the Coming of the Civil War.* New York: Knopf Doubleday, 1997.

Lavaca Commercial, Port Lavaca, Texas.

McComb, David G. *Texas, A Modern History.* Austin: University of Texas Press, 1989.

McKenzie, Phyllis A. "Margaret Heffernan Borland," in *Texas Women on the Cattle Trails,* edited by Sara R. Massey. College Station: Texas A&M University Press, 2006.

McLean, John H. "Our Early Schools," *Texas Methodist Historical Quarterly* 2, no. 1 (July 1910).

McLean, Margaret. "Tournaments: An Account of This Early Sport in Victoria, Texas and Neighboring Communities." *The Cattleman,* September 1, 1948.

McLean, Margaret Stoner. "Rose, William Pinckney." *Handbook of Texas Online,* August 17, 2014, http://www.tshaonline.org/handbook/online/articles/fr074.

McLemore, Laura Lyons. *Inventing Texas: Early Historians of the Lone Star State.* College Station: Texas A&M University Press, 2004.

McNutt, James C. "Borland, Margaret Heffernan." *Handbook of Texas Online,* August 20, 2014, http://www.tshaonline.org/handbook/online/articles/fb072.

Moneyhon, Carl H. *Texas after the Civil War: The Struggle of Reconstruction.* College Station: Texas A&M University Press, 2004.

Morgan, Lee. *Centenary College of Louisiana, 1825–2000: The Biography of an American Academy.* Shreveport: Centenary College of Louisiana Press, 2008.

Morris, Leopold. *Pictorial History of Victoria and Victoria County.* San Antonio: Clemons Printing, 1953.

Myers, Lois. *Letters by Lamplight.* Waco, TX: Baylor University Press, 1991.

Myers, Lois E. "Oral Memoirs of Mary Margaret Stoner McLean." Family Life and Community History Project—Baylor University Institute for Oral History, 2010.

Myrtle Springs Herald, Myrtle Springs, Texas.

Needham, Julia Rose Brooking. "The Brookings," submitted by Dorothy N. Whitley. *True West Magazine,* June 1976.

"Old Subscribers of the News: Mr. J.W. Rose of Kelly, N.M., A Reader of the News for Many Years." *Galveston Daily News,* September 14, 1895.

Pavković, Aleksandar, and Peter Radan. *Creating New States; Theory and Practice of Secession,* Farnham, UK: Ashgate Publishing, 2007.

Petty, J. W. Jr., ed. *A Republishing of the Book Most Often Known as Victor Rose's History of Victoria.* Victoria, TX: Book Mart, 1961.

Record and Matriculation Book, 1852–1907, 65, Student Records, Centenary College of Louisiana Archives and Special Collections, Shreveport, Louisiana.

Ridgely, J. V. "The Confederacy and the Martyred South." In *Nineteenth-Century Southern Literature*. Lexington: The University Press of Kentucky, 1980.

Roberts, Giselle. "Sewing for the Soldiers." In *The Confederate Belle*. Columbia: University Press of Missouri, 2003.

Roell, Craig H. "Linn, John Joseph." *Handbook of Texas Online*, May 13, 2014, http://www.tshaonline.org/handbook/online/articles/fli12.

———. "Rose, Victor Marion." *Handbook of Texas Online*, October 28, 2013, http://www.tshaonline.org/handbook/online/articles/fr073.

———. "Crain, William Henry." *Handbook of Texas Online*, May 10, 2017, http://www.tshaonline.org/handbook/online/articles/fcr01.

Rose, Victor M. *Celeste Valcœur: A Legend of Dixie*. Philadelphia: Pictorial Bureau of the Press, 1886.

———. *Demara, the Comanche Queen; and Other Rhymes*. New York: J. J. Little & Co., 1882.

———. Letter to Margaret Rose, May 20, 1861 (digital image), Centenary College of Louisiana Archives, Shreveport, Louisiana.

———. *Los Despenadores—A Spanish Story*. Austin: State Book & Job Office, 1878.

———. *Ross' Texas Brigade: Being a Narrative of Events Connected with Its Service in the Late War between the States*. Louisville: Courier-Journal Book and Job Rooms, 1881.

———. *Stephen F. Austin, In the Balances*. n.p., 1890.

———. *The Life and Services of Gen. Ben McCulloch*. Philadelphia: Pictorial Bureau of the Press, 1888; facs. ed., Austin: Steck Company, 1858.

———. *The Texas Vendetta; or, The Sutton-Taylor Feud*. New York: J. J. Little & Co., 1880.

———. *While the Spell of Her Witchery Lingers, and Other Poems*. Laredo, TX: n.p., 1886.

Sansing, David G. *The University of Mississippi: A Sesquicentennial History*. Jackson: University Press of Mississippi, 1999.

Shaw Jr., Arthur M. *Centenary College Goes to War in 1861*. Shreveport: Centenary College, 1940.

Sinks, Julia Lee. "Rutersville College." *Quarterly of the Texas State Historical Association* 2, no. 2 (1898).

Southwestern Historical Quarterly 66 (July 1962).

State of Texas v. Victor M. Rose and Charles T. Wilson, No. 357. District Court, Victoria County, Texas, August 23, 1860. Victoria Regional History Center, VC/UHV Library, Victoria, Texas.

Stoner, Zilpa Rose. "Life of Zilpa Rose Stoner." August 1, 1930, Victoria County Archives, Victoria, Texas.

Texian Advocate, Victoria, Texas.

The Laredo Times, Laredo, Texas.

The Old Capitol, Columbia, Texas.

The Weekly Advocate, Victoria, Texas.

Utley, Robert M. *Lone Star Justice: The First Century of the Texas Rangers*. Oxford and New York: Oxford University Press, 2002.

Victoria Advocate, Victoria, Texas.

"Victoria County Deed Records." Victoria County Courthouse, Victoria, Texas.

"Victoria County Probate Minutes." Victoria County Courthouse, Victoria, Texas.

Waxahachie Enterprise, Waxahachie, Texas.

Weekly Democratic Statesman, Austin, Texas.

Weisiger, Sidney R. "Grist Mills of This Area." *Victoria Advocate*, May 10, 1970.

Williams, Amelia W. "Paschal, George Washington." *Handbook of Texas Online*, http://www.tshaonline.org/handbook/online/articles/fpa46.

Winkler, Ernest William, ed. *Journal of the Secession Convention of Texas 1861*. https://archive.org/details/journalofsecessi00texarich.

Woodworth, Steven E. *Jefferson Davis and His Generals: The Failure of the Confederate Command in the West*. Lawrence: University Press of Kansas, 1990.

Zott, Lynn M., ed. "Literature of the Antebellum South—C. Alphonso Smith (Essay Date 1908)." *Nineteenth-Century Literary Criticism*, vol. 112. Farmington Hills, MI: Gale Cengage, 2002. Accessed August 19, 2013, http://www.enotes.com/literature-antebellum-south-essays/literature-antebellum-south/c-alphonso-smith-essay-date-1908.

———, ed. "Literature of the Antebellum South—Introduction." *Nineteenth-Century Literary Criticism*, vol. 112. Farmington Hills, MI: Gale Cengage, 2002. Accessed October 8, 2012, http://www.enotes.com/topics/literature-antebellum-south#critical-essays-literature-antebellum-south-introduction.

———, ed. "Literature of the Antebellum South—J.V. Ridgely (Essay Date 1980)." *Nineteenth-Century Literary Criticism*, vol. 112. Farmington Hills, MI: Gale Cengage, 2002. Accessed October 8, 2012, http://www.enotes.com/literature-antebellum-south-criticism/literature-antebellum-south/j-v-ridgely-essay-date-1980.

———, ed. "Literature of the Antebellum South—Jan Bakker (Essay Date 1986)." *Nineteenth-Century Literary Criticism*, vol. 112. Farmington Hills, MI: Gale Cengage, 2002. Accessed September 16, 2012, http://www.enotes.com/literature-antebellum-south-criticism/literature-antebellum-south/jan-bakker-essay-date-1986.

———, ed. "Literature of the Antebellum South—Lewis P. Simpson (Essay Date 1973)." *Nineteenth-Century Literary Criticism*, vol. 112. Farmington Hills, MI: Gale Cengage, 2002. Accessed October 9, 2012, http://www.enotes.com/literature-antebellum-south-criticism/literature-antebellum-south/lewis-p-simpson-essay-date-1973.

———, ed. "Literature of the Antebellum South—Richard Gray (Essay Date 1986)." *Nineteenth-Century Literary Criticism*, vol. 112. Farmington Hills, MI:

Gale Cengage, 2002. Accessed August 19, 2013, http://www.enotes.com/lit
erature-antebellum-south-essays/literature-antebellum-south/richard-gray-
essay-date-1986.

———, ed. "Literature of the Antebellum South—Thomas Nelson Page (Essay
Date 1892)." *Nineteenth-Century Literary Criticism*, vol. 112. Farmington Hills,
MI: Gale Cengage, 2002. Accessed October 8, 2012, http://www.enotes.com/lit
erature-antebellum-south-essays/literature-antebellum-south/thomas-nelson-
page-essay-date-1892.

INDEX